ISBN: 978-0-9903097-2-7

ARDNEK Publishing, LLC.

www.ardnekpublishing.com

Richmond, Virginia

DEDICATED TO

My father, Antonio "Tony" Leonard Esparza, his vision and mission work, Image Church, and my sister, Monica Esparza and the Renewal of Life Trust, for keeping it going.

ACKNOWLEDGMENTS

I would like to first acknowledge all of the young readers. Renewal of mind will carry you far so don't ever stop reading and learning! I continue to remain humbled by the amount of letters and comments you share and thank you, your parents, guardians, community and schools for your continued love and support!

Thank you to my editor, Sam Kruit, of Bowler Fern, LTD for her work on all three books in the series. A special acknowledgment to my niece, Catherine (Cat Karma) for her extraordinary work on the illustrations for the characters and her work on my children's illustrated book, "Raja's College Life, A True Story." So proud of your drive and pursuits. Thank you to my sister, Melody, for sitting beside me at all those events and looking fab! Thank you to Kendra for telling it like it is and assisting in keeping my affairs straight. Thank you to my sister, Monica, for her book formatting and carrying out our dad's life work with the Renewal of Life Trust.

CONTENTS

Chapter 1

Sage slouched down in the pew, her hands wrinkling her beige linen skirt. She pressed the tops of her shoes on the floor as she rapidly tapped her feet together, making her shoes begin to slide off the back of her heels.

Sage put her hand up to her mouth to cover her yawn. She thought about falling asleep for a quick moment. If only her Nana didn't like the early bird service so much, maybe she wouldn't mind coming. Not only did Sage have to sit for two hours during service, she'd also had to get up at the crack of dawn which she never liked doing, especially on a day she didn't have to be in school.

Nana returned from one of her social chats and squeezed Sage down along the pew. "Sit up like a lady!" Nana whispered.

Sage straightened up at her Nana's urging and looked down at her lap. Sage's skirt was now wrinkly enough to embarrass even her. She sucked her teeth, waiting impatiently for service to begin.

Sage was not a regular at church, nor did she want to be. She made it occasionally, but only because of her Nana. She knew her Nana well enough to know that too many 'no's' would eventually end up coming back to haunt her; Nana would lose patience and make her go every Sunday on principle alone.

No way was she getting up *this* early every Sunday.

She thought back to how comfortable her bed had been this morning as she'd lain with her legs hanging off the sides of the bed and her body half covered up in her bright pink blanket. As sleepy as she'd been, she had been thinking about wrestling Nana at the moment she walked in to wake her.

Sage giggled at the thought of jumping up out of the blanket and grabbing hold of her grandmother with all her wrinkles and her creaky bones. She could see Nana's shock and hear her cry of, "Lor' chile!"

"Shh!" Nana gave her a hard nudge and 'the look.'

Sage crossed her arms across her chest and stopped the giggle, looking around the church to distract herself. It was small, but clean and decorated nicely. The walls were painted the palest possible tint of grey. Once, when her Nana had described the renovation of the little chapel, Sage had thought that grey walls sounded awful. But it was peaceful, she realized, looking around and the grey shade didn't compete with the arches and stained glass windows. Sage eyes rested on her favorite window covered in several shades of blue with a yellow cross in the center surrounded by vines and a dove. Sage heard music and looked towards the back of the church to see the youth choir as they came stepping into the church singing.

Sage warmed to this part of the church service. Nana's church had about 100 members. They had what Sage liked to call the Ladies in Blue choir, the Men in Black choir, the Old Folk's choir and the Young Folk's choir. Nana had talked Sage into church this morning by saying, "come on chile, it's the third Sunday. The Youth choir's gonna sing today." Sage couldn't keep up with the second, third and fourth Sundays, but her Nana seemed to have the pattern embedded in her brain or something. For Sage, the best Sundays where when the Youth choir sang or when she took open communion. For some odd reason, she always looked forward to that little bit of cracker and grape juice, not that she'd ever let Nana hear her say *that* again. Years ago, she'd reported back on a service to her mom (whose two jobs meant she attended church even less often than Sage did), sharing how she really liked the story of how the Apostle Peter got his strength back, and getting the grape juice and crackers at the end. Her Nana had gasped like she'd been dropped in ice water. "Chile! Don't you call the body and blood of Jesus Christ, our Lord and Savior, no crackers and grape juice! Lor', I do wonder about this chile sometimes…" Sage had become subjected to weeklong scripture readings to make sure she was worthy to receive the body and blood of Christ in the future.

Sage looked up at the choir, who'd just arrived in their places. Darren Timberlake towered over everyone else. Darren was one of the coolest guys in her school, with one of the best voices she'd ever heard. He was also the guy nobody really knew anything about. Sage was always trying to get up the nerve to say something to him, and telling herself she had to join the youth choir to be near him. To this day, she still hadn't spoken to him—or joined the choir. That was probably for the best, though. She couldn't sing, though she spent days, hours and weeks wishing she could.

Sage didn't feel she really had a talent, unless you counted the kind coming from your hands. She played a soprano saxophone and flute, and could learn a new instrument in a matter of months. She could also make up tunes and beats without much thought, an ability the school teacher seemed to be amazed by, but then again, the music department wasn't very good so his opinion didn't carry much weight with her

She just wished she had real talent like Beyonce, Mary J Blige and Jennifer Hudson. Glam and glitter with dance moves to kill was what she wanted. If she could be like them, everybody would be hollerin' at her, wantin' to know her name and be near her.

The choir began singing "I'd rather have Jesus than Silver and Gold." They sounded like they could make a gospel album. While enjoying the music, rocking her head to it, Sage scanned the rest of the choir group. She noticed a few other people from her neighborhood and school, including her closest friend Melanie James, who was looking out at the congregation and singing her heart out. The James' were devoted members of the church so Melanie didn't have a choice on whether she got up on a Sunday or not.

The choir faded out *Silver and Gold* and launched into *Wanna Be Happy* swaying from side to side and looking so relaxed and confident in their burgundy robes. Sage's eyes landed on Gina Conner, a fellow student at her school. Sage felt a tinge of jealousy just looking over at her. Gina was one of those happy people who always seemed busy making the world her oyster. Sage had even seen her with Darren Timberlake at Skate World last school year, the pair of them gliding around the rink, hand in hand. Sage and her friends had stood there, dumbstruck, wondering how she'd managed to make that happen. She'd probably just smiled her perfect smile at him. Sage didn't hate Gina, but the girl seemed annoyingly…together. The service began with its usual order with Sage letting out a couple of more yarns through-out.

The Pastor got up and walked to the pulpit giving his amen's for the Youth choir, their beautiful voices and another glorious day in the house of the Lord. Though short, the pastor looked mighty big behind that pulpit. Sage always thought he looked and sounded like he could be a teacher. He wasn't one of those preachers who made the Bible sound like a foreign language. She'd been to churches with pastors like that and had literally fallen asleep, mid-sermon.

He cleared his throat, declared that the theme of the day's sermon was accepting God's gifts with grace. Sage half-listened. She recognized the shape of the story about Timothy, the Apostle Paul's protégé, a diamond in the rough. But then the pastor talked about laying hands on one hastingly which lost her. She didn't recognize that part and half lost stopped paying attention.

"And no," the pastor shouted. Sage came back to attention with his loud proclamation. There will be no squandering of God's special gift through Christ, Our Lord Savior. Right, let's open our bibles at…"

Sage fumbled her way to 1 Timothy, Chapter 4 … something, but lost the last verse. She looked over at her Nana so she could ask her what he'd said but Nana looked totally engrossed. Sage gave up trying find the passage and just looked forward. Before long, she'd blocked out most of what the pastor was saying and had gone into a trance of her own.

In her day-dream, Sage was beautiful like the performers she idolized. She had thick hair she could braid easily, and didn't need any makeup. She had a closet full of great clothes and never wondered how she was going to fit in with what style. Today, she had on a DKNY black tailored cotton suit with a cute white tee and a dog-chain necklace. She was on stage, next to Darren Timberlake, having been asked to duet with him on the most popular song of the year. She and Darren sang their hearts out. They finished and he smiled at her and gave her a hug. She turned back to the audience, who were giving them a standing ovation.

Sage was beaming at the audience, when she felt a hard nudge from Darren. She turned to him, startled to see Nana looking back at her.

Sage crouched down, embarrassed. Something had made Nana aware that she wasn't paying attention, but she didn't know what. Did some kind of neon sign switch on over her head when she was day-dreaming? Sage turned to her Nana, smiling sheepishly, and got the other 'look' which *really* made her straighten up. Sage looked at her Bible as if she knew what verse they were on and sat up. That seemed to satisfy her Nana, who turned back to the Pastor.

Sage knew she had a bad habit of 'taking temporary leave from the real world,' as her Nana would say. She was always putting herself in another place or body—anyone's but her own.

Her friends were always trying to convince her that her body and face were nice, but she didn't believe them. Truth be known, Sage didn't think she was all that bad looking; she was just plain average in every way: average face, an average body, average hair and average grades. She figured she didn't need to have everything; she definitely wanted great hair, and would probably work harder for great grades if she felt everything else was going her way.

Sage shifted a little in the pew and glanced up at the pulpit, to find the pastor was looking smack dab at her. She felt so uncomfortable she quickly looked away, fixing her gaze on the Bible which was still open and unread in her lap. The pastor was getting excited about "seeing something, but trusting in something." It made no sense to Sage, but since she hadn't been paying attention, that didn't come as a surprise. She rubbed the back of her neck like it was sore, a habit she'd developed if she thought she was in trouble. She glanced up quickly and nearly jumped; now he seemed to *really* be studying her, standing on his tip toes and leaning over the pulpit as if he wanted to climb on top. She turned away from his stare, but could still feel his eyes on her.

"You see?" he said excitedly, "… says do not neglect the gifts that are in you! It doesn't matter if you feel you are too young, too old, don't feel you are good enough, you've got to have faith and trust in what God has entrusted in you."

Sage shrunk down in her seat, feeling like he was delivering this sermon just for her.

"God gives us all gifts and by trusting in that gift and using it you can reach heights beyond your imagination. Are you not going to trust these gifts to make a way when nothing seems to be going your way? Open your eyes, trust and nurture what God gives you!" he preached. "You got to stop lookin' out for something that don't mean nothing!"

People stood up in the aisle, their hands raised.

Sage looked back at the pulpit, but the pastor didn't seem to be looking at her anymore. He was wiping his forehead with a handkerchief and looking down at the Bible. Relieved, Sage settled back to watch everyone getting excited about his sermon. Sage had a theory that the crowds at church acted the same way during each sermon and had shared this with Melanie.

"Watch," Sage had said. "The pastor's going to start talking with early nods and hummm-ummm's from everybody. Then you'll hear an occasional amen and hallelujah. After a while, the thirty to fifty somethin' crowd will start standing up and clapping with their arms raised. The elders and children just sit there."

"That's not true," Melanie had defended. "You don't even go to church enough to know."

Sage looked up at the choir now and met Melanie's eyes, then turned away, smirking. When the service was done, she'd brag that she was right, and that Melanie knew it. This had been the fifth sermon since that conversation and it always ended the same way.

The highlight for Sage was the benediction, the ending of service. She couldn't wait to get out of the pew and into the yard. That's where most of the kids her age hung out afterwards . The church service ended and Sage's landscape became a maze of huge hats with even bigger feathers than Nana's as the congregation got to their feet. Sage told her Nana that she was going out to the yard, and at her nod of approval started to walk out of the chapel.

Sage couldn't shake off the feeling the Pastor had been staring right at her, but couldn't figure out why. God hadn't given her the gift to sing, so it wasn't like she was wasting anything. God should've given her a voice like Beyonce so she could make some M-O-N-E-Y.

In the yard, a few kids were already standing around talking while turning their cell phones on. Sage knew all but two of them and as she walked past them, looking for Melanie, heard her name called.

"Sage," Lisa called. "Do you know when tryouts for the talent show will be held?"

"Um…" Sage was a little nervous her answer would be wrong; the thought of being mistaken when Lisa asked a question was just flat-out scary. Lisa, one of the tallest and biggest girls at East Grandell Middle, could be overbearing. Sage cleared her throat. "I think it's this Tuesday."

"Told you, Lisa!" one of the other girls said, quickly turning back to her phone screen. The group started to talk among themselves about what they might do while Sage stood awkwardly to the side, not knowing if she should stay or continue walking. Lisa dominated the group and conversation. When they were at school, Lisa always acted like a bully, pushing past people with teachers constantly having to tell her to be polite, move over or go see the Principal. Not only did she look tough, but she talked like she hadn't learned any other words except those that your mama taught you not to say. Sage was always puzzled to see her at church; she was one of the regulars, too. Sage was always left wondering how someone could go to church each and every Sunday but spend Monday through Saturday "raisin' up the devil", as her Nana would say.

With what seemed like an eternity of awkwardness, Sage backed away from the group and walked away. She scanned the yard, but no Melanie.

Gina waved. "Hey Sage, I overheard you all talking about tryouts. Are you going to try out?"

Sage wished she could say, 'Yes, Darren and I will be singing together.' Instead she replied, "Hey Gina and not sure what I'd tryout with."

Gina shrugged. "I hope you audition so I can hear you play that sax."

Sage shrugged. "I'm thinking about it."

Sage then saw Melanie coming around the side of the church, walking between her parents.

Sage pulled away from Gina, waving down Melanie and fell into step with her as they crossed the yard over to the gate, away from the eavesdropping ears of adults. She grinned at her buddy and folded her arms. "Five sermons and counting."

Melanie acted like she didn't hear Sage, looking up and around as if there was a voice coming out of the air. "I don't SEE NOTHIN' OR

HEAR NOTHIN'!"

Sage laughed. Seems someone was paying attention in church.

"What's everyone talking about over there?" said Melanie.

"Tryouts for the talent show."

"So, what are you going to be doing?"

"Who says I'm doing anything? I can't sing and I'm not that great of a dancer either."

Melanie looked at her with an expression of amazement. "You can play that sax of yours with your eyes closed. Don't you want to try out playing your instrument? You could actually write your own song."

"No one wants to hear that, Melanie. My Nana's been making me play it for years and even I don't want to hear it. Anyway, who always gets the attention? It's the people who can sing, not the ones providing the tunes."

"Who've you been talking to?" Melanie looked at Sage with her mouth open in frozen shock.

Sage looked back at Melanie with her hand on her hip and a long hard stare. Close your mouth and stop looking at me like that."

"I'll keep my mouth open if I want to, but back to you. I want to know why you care who gets attention and when? We're talking about your talent, not people's attention. You are GOOD!"

"But—" Sage noticed Darren Timberlake walking towards them. She adjusted her stance and put her hand up to her hair to make sure it was in place.

Melanie noticed her fidgeting and looked over her shoulder to see

Darren walking up to them. She turned. "Hey, Darren."

"Hey." Darren produced a folded sheet of paper from his back pocket, and a pen. "I'm just taking a vote. Mr. Chandler wants to change choir rehearsal to Thursday to avoid clashing with the Tuesday tryouts for the talent show. He wanted me to check with you to see if that day is okay."

"Sure it is. I'll tell my mom."

"Alright, I'll let him know." Darren made a note on his sheet then looked right at Sage, his eyes kind. "You go to EG Middle too, right? How are you?"

"Fine" was all she could get out. She wanted to kick herself.

"Are you trying out for the talent show too?"

"Yes," Sage blurted, wanting to see more of that friendly sparkle in his eyes. "What about you?"

"I'm thinking about it. What are you going to do?"

"Mmmm, I'm thinking about ballet or singing."

"Get out! You know ballet?"

Melanie stared at Sage. "What?"

"Yeah, a little, I learned it as a child."

Darren grinned. "This is so cool. Nobody does ballet these days."

"Well, I'm not saying I'm good—"

Melanie snorted. "Neither is anyone else!"

Sage sidestepped, putting Melanie right behind her shoulder so she didn't have to see her jaw drop again. Much as she loved her friend, she wished Melanie were far away, right now. Siberia would be good.

"My aunt is a ballerina in the Washington Dance Company," Darren said excitedly. "I'll have to try out just to see you dance!" He checked his watch. "See you guys later. I need to get back to Mr. Chandler."

When Darren got out of range, Melanie lit into her friend. "Why did you tell that big lie?"

"I don't know," Sage admitted. "It just came out."

"Just… came… out?" Melanie shook her head in disbelief. "It took some work in those brain cells to come up with that one!"

Sage felt her stomach getting tight. She didn't understand what had gotten into her. She just wanted him to think of her as special and different and… it just came out. Besides, she wasn't lying about doing ballet when she was younger. She'd taken classes for two years when she was five and six years old. She remembered a little bit of it. Maybe she could get a refresher somewhere over the weekend. Well, she had to do something. He really seemed impressed and the thought of coming clean just made her blood run cold.

Sage looked up and saw her Nana waving her hand to come on. She'd never been so relieved to have an adult call her away from something. "My Nana's leaving so I'm out."

"Okay Ms. Ballerina." Melanie was still shaking her head when she turned to walk away.

Sage wondered how she was going to be able to get a routine together before Tuesday. If she could get to the mall, she could get into a bookstore or get a video-tape, or something. She just needed to jog her muscle memory.

Chapter 2

Sage was fuming. It was almost two in the afternoon and her mother was still in bed. Sage wondered how someone could sleep all day long. She and Nana had gone to church, come home, eaten lunch and tidied the family section of the living room (half of it was Nana's bedroom), and mom was *still* in bed.

Right now, Sage needed her mother to take her to the mall. She'd asked Nana, but knew that had been a long shot. Nana believed Sundays were for church, Sunday dinner and rest. She was in the kitchen working on dinner now. Sage smiled though, hearing the pots and pans being banged around. She liked having her Nana around. She'd moved in a year ago when it became too difficult for her to stay in her apartment—something about the social security no longer taking care of it. When Sage came home from school, Nana was there with a sandwich, love and a smile. When it was time for her to go to bed, Nana was usually the one tucking her in with a kiss. Before Nana had moved in, it was Sage winging it alone. When her mother wasn't working one of her two jobs, she was sleeping from exhaustion.

Sage pushed her way into her mother's room to see her all sprawled out on the bed like an eagle.

Wake up. Wake up!

Sage looked down at her mother, trying to reach her mind with her thoughts as if this would do the trick. As much as she needed to get her ballet research stuff, she wasn't ready to upset her mom by shaking her. She looked so peaceful, asleep.

Looking down, Sage wondered why she, herself, looked so average when her mother was an absolute beauty with the prettiest skin ever—like poured milk chocolate. She wore her hair cut short and close and the waves in her hair seemed to lie in all the right places. Sage's hair came past her shoulders and it seemed she could never get it into the styles she wanted. Her hair was wavy like her mother's, but her mom would never let her cut it, telling her how beautiful it was long.

Sage's mom was also petite: Sage was the complete opposite, taller by nearly a foot and still only in the seventh grade. Sage's caramel-colored skin had little pimples all over it. Nana kept telling her the pimples came from all the soda she drank, but she was sure it was some bad gene from her father, a man she'd never met.

The only thing her mother seemed to have passed on was her book smarts, though Sage never much used hers. Her mom had graduated in the top of her class and had big plans to be a doctor, even getting a four-year scholarship at some big school. As Nana explained things, Sage had 'happened' right before she was supposed to go. Sage always heard Nana trying to get her to go back to college. Mom would get ready, but never seemed to find the time. Nana would always respond with, "If you'd stop drowning your past decisions in those jobs of yours, you might find the time." Sage never asked what she meant by that, but did know she didn't want to be in that situation when she graduated from school. She didn't have to know all the details to know it made her mother miserable.

She flopped down on the edge of the bed, which made her mother move. Sage looked over to see her mom actually coming to life.

Sage's mom opened her eyes. They were almond shaped and brown, long-lashed and seemed just right against her skin, even when she was waking up and ought to look terrible. Sage felt lower than ever.

"Hey Baby."

"Hi Ma."

Her mom frowned, squeezing Sage's hand. "You okay?"

"No, I need to get to the mall—today—and I need you to take me before they close. Nana won't take me."

Her mom stretched and looked over at her clock. "What do you need to get to the mall for?"

"I need a book on ballet for school."

"Ballet?" Her mom's eyebrows shot up. "Your school has you studying ballet?"

"No." She didn't want to offer more so she put as much attitude into it as she dared without getting in trouble.

"You just said you needed it for school and can't you get a book in the library?"

"It's complicated, but I need it today!" Sage whined while putting on a distressed face.

"Remember how much you hated ballet when I had you taking lessons?"

"No, I didn't. I just didn't like the teacher."

Sage's mom raised her eyebrow yet again, but instead of digging any deeper said, "I can take you. Let me get out of bed and get myself together."

Wow—that was easy. Sage leapt off the bed and kissed her mother.

"Thanks, Ma."

Sage skipped out of her mom's room, figuring out what she could do in the half-hour or so it would take her mom to get ready. She needed to actually watch some ballet. There was always something showing just about every time she flicked through the channels looking for a cartoon or video show. She went into the living room and started going through the shelves up under the TV stand. Magazines, newspapers and old guides were now neatly piled on top of each other. She pulled the latest guide and sat on the couch, thumbing through until she found a listing for 'La Bayadere', starting in another hour. She went to her own room to set the recorder.

As half the living room was now Nana's bedroom—her part blocked off with a partition—Sage now had the rights to TV in her own room. Her room was her haven; everything she needed was in there. It was crowded though, because she wasn't so good at chucking stuff out—

Maybe she still had her old ballet stuff?

Her old ballet costumes and shoes were probably still in her kindergarten box. While she knew she couldn't fit any of that stuff anymore, holding it in her hands might at least bring back memories. Sage opened the doors carefully—she didn't want anything spilling out on her head.

The closet was as crowded as her room. The outfits weren't in the box she thought they'd be in, so she knelt down on the floor and began moving things around to see if she could find the costumes or leotard hiding under the pile of clothes that she'd meant to put out for Goodwill. She stayed on her knees for a good fifteen minutes with no success. Just where did she put that stuff? *Had* she even kept it?

Her mother had been right about her hating the ballet. At the time, she felt like all her friends were doing everything else fun while she was being made to take those stupid lessons. Her mother and Nana had made her take them for two years thinking it would eventually grow on her, but she'd just gotten more and more resentful. Now she'd wished she'd continued.

What if she'd kept trying? Would she have blossomed? Maybe she'd have improved year-on-year until she was being asked to help the instructor teach the new girls in her spare time. Maybe people from other dance companies would've heard of her.

Sage settled on her knees by the closet and imagined a chance meeting with Darren's aunt.

In her mind, Darren's aunt looked like a ballerina. She also looked like Darren, except she was prettier and of course much smaller. Sage pictured them walking side by side coming towards her while she was on the stage, doing her stretches and getting ready for tryouts.

Darren smiled. "Sage, I'd like you to meet my aunt. I told her how good you were in ballet. She wanted to come down and see you try out."

Sage shook his aunt's hand, full of confidence. "I really appreciate that. When I finish, could we talk about different techniques?"

"Sage," yelled the stagehand, "You're up."

"Could you dim the lights?" she called back. She pointed to Foster, a thin and frail boy she felt bad for at school. He'd begged Sage to let him help her with her show and she'd finally put him in charge of turning the music on and off so he'd leave her alone. The audience fell silent as she began very gracefully extending her leg out from under her.

"Sage?"

Sage jumped and looked up to see who was interrupting her show. Her mother was standing at the door.

"Didn't you hear me calling you? Are you ready to go to the mall?"

"Oh! Yeah, I was trying to find something in the closet."

"You might find it if you actually look instead of staring into space." Sage's mom rolled her eyes and walked out of the room.

Sage pushed herself up off the floor and hurriedly put on her shoes. She rushed through the living room and into the kitchen, where her mother was talking to Nana. Nana was listening while still busy at dinner. Sage was sure Nana just liked standing in the kitchen. Even if the food was sitting in the oven or simmering on the stove, Nana was standing right over it, opening pots and doing her many tastings. The few times Sage had cooked, she'd walked away from the stove and sat down in the living room to watch TV. Twice she'd burned the bottom of the pot, and she had only been heating up ravioli from the can.

"I'm ready," Sage said, walking towards the door. "Bye, Nana."

"Bye Baby, dinner'll be ready when you get back."

Sage loved the way her Nana ran words together. She smiled, waved her hand and stepped outside in the hallway. She and her mom took the stairs of the apartment down to the parking lot and headed over to the car, an old Toyota Supra. One of her mom's old boyfriends had given her the car a few years back. It had over 100,000 miles on it, but it still ran good.

"Which mall are we going to?" her mother asked.

"Northside Mall has the book and video stores, so let's go there."

They were backing out of the parking space when Sage's mom began her inquisition. "Now, what class do you need this for?"

"I don't need it for a class," Sage responded, not providing any more information than that.

"I thought you said you needed it for school."

"I do need it for school, just not a class at school. It's… part of my personal development.." She picked at a hole in the cuff of her sleeve.

Sage's mother looked over at her with a look of confusion, but quickly turned back to the road.

"That doesn't make sense to me, Sage. What are you talking about?"

While Sage could create little white lies with people she didn't know very well, lying to her mother was another story. She couldn't repeat the lie she'd created for Darren. She breathed out hard. "I didn't want to go into much detail, but since you insist on knowing—"

"Attitude, Sage!"

"Sorry." She shuffled in her seat, not wanting her mom to turn round and go home. "I wanted to try out for the talent show this year."

Her mother was quiet for a moment. "What has that got to do with a book on ballet?'

"I was going to do a dance for the try out and wanted to review the techniques again."

"Girl, have you lost your mind?"

"Why do you say that? This is something different that I want to try."

Sage's mom took a hard corner, shaking her head. "Sage, a talent show is put on to display people's talents, to showcase people who excel at something. It's not a stage for trying new things. Why don't you play your sax or the flute? Now that's talent."

Sage crossed her arms and looked out the car window. She was sick and tired of hearing people say she should play the sax or flute. Nobody seemed to want to hear it any time she was actually playing, but now all of a sudden everybody thought she should play for the talent show. Plus, she'd already told Darren Timberlake she was going to do ballet and he'd gotten really excited. She knew if she did this right, people at the school would look at her differently—especially him.

They drove the rest of the way with only the car radio making sounds, pulling into the parking lot of Northside Mall in silence, Sage was still staring out the window as if there was something actually happening out there. Sage's mom found a parking space close to the Barnes and Noble store and cut the engine off. Sage knew her mother was looking her way now.

"Sage" her mother said, "Look at me, girl."

Sage turned to her mother, but couldn't look her in the eyes.

"For some reason, you're always trying to be something other than what you are. You have a beautiful smile, but never see it. You're tall like a model, but want to be short. Your hair waves and curls like the ocean, but you want it straight. Most of all, you have a gift to make music that most children your age could only ever dream of, but you see it as day ole bread. You need to open your eyes and celebrate who you are, instead of giving homage to those things you're not."

Sage lifted her eyes to her mother's, but didn't say anything. Her mother sighed and opened the car door.

"Do you have money for this book?" her mom asked.

"Yeah."

"I'm going to go into Nordstrom's and look around. Do you have your cell on you?"

"Yeah, I'll call you after I find the book."

"Fine."

Sage thought about what her mother said while she made her way to the front door of Barnes and Noble. Of course, her mother would think those nice things about her since she was her mother. But then again, some of the things she had said did ring true—in a small way. Sage found her way through to the Arts section. After looking through the ballet books for about half an hour, Sage did begin to wonder if she should change to music for the tryouts. The positions looked challenging.

She remembered feeling very uncomfortable trying to strike those poses. Plus, although she had a leotard and wrap-skirt she could use, she would need to buy those special shoes. She hadn't thought about that part. That would take half of her money. Sage socked away any money she got for birthdays, chores around the house or any money she got when Nana or her mother were just being generous with "keep the change." She didn't buy much so she had a good amount saved up, but she'd need to find the shoes today. Her heart sank.

Sage sat on one of the armchairs in the reading area and thought hard about how she could get the shoes. Nothing came to her. After all, she couldn't ask her mother to take her to a costume store—her mom already thought she was losing her mind by buying a book. She'd put her foot down if she knew Sage was going to spend more than $20.00 on these tryouts. Asking Nana was out of the question.

Undeterred, Sage sighed. She'd have to try out without the shoes and use her sneakers. Sage looked down at the books she'd pulled out and chose the one on classical ballet. It was what she'd studied as a child, and the book had a lot of illustrations in it that helped. By the time she'd made her way to the cash register to pay for the book, she felt energized and excited with her decision to go through with this. She'd almost faltered when her mother was lecturing in the car. She paid for the book and, a few minutes later, found her mother in Nordstrom's petite casual section.

She was holding up a spandex dress with leopard print at the top and solid black towards the bottom. Sage thought about lecturing her mother on her dressing habits, but knew she'd get knocked out if she even tried. Her mom's size was the only thing petite about her. She had a tall voice, a tall personality and a strong hold in that small little fist of hers.

"Oh, hey hon. What do you think of this one?"

"Uh…it's petite but maybe not so…casual."

"Afraid to tell me it's too young, right?" Her mom laughed and put the dress back. "Don't worry—I was just checking out the shape. I'm not so hot on V-necks, anyway."

"Right." Sage trailed behind as her mom drifted over to a different rack and pulled out two hangers. She checked her watch. It was five after three, already. She whimpered inside. What about her practice time? She wanted to get home and start practicing.

"Mom—"

"Huh?"

Her mom gave her a lop-sided smile. "Since you're all about making your own grown-up decisions, you may as well start calling me Pam. Or would that be too weird?"

Sage felt maybe it would be. But then, her Nana did most of the 'mom' things anyway. And maybe thinking of her mom as 'Pam' might make them closer again. She shrugged. "I'll try."

"It's not about trying. It's about what you want to do. It's about doing what's right for *you*."

Sage didn't answer that because she knew it was a not-so-subtle hint her mom was adding to her earlier lecture. She figured maybe this 'Pam' thing was a test and decided she'd go for it; especially with her needing to move along. She smiled and followed 'Pam' to the next rack of clothes. She was determined to stay cool, hoping 'Pam' would finish her walk around Nordstroms soon.

Chapter 3

Finally they were back in the car headed home.

By the time Pam announced she didn't see anything worth buying, Sage had been reduced to following her around like a Zombie. She was convinced Pam was out to torture her for wanting to practice ballet by wasting their whole afternoon. Her stomach rumbled; she had eaten half of a peanut butter and jelly sandwich her Nana had prepared when they'd gotten back home from church, but nothing else. She always made sure to save lots of room for Nana's Sunday dinners, which they usually ate around four. It was a little after four, right now.

"I'm going to stuff my face when I get home," laughed Sage.

"You and me both," Pam said.

Sage couldn't help but ask the question she always kept in the back of her head. Her mother worked a lot so she didn't get to spend a whole lot of time talking to her. "Ma—Pam—did Nana ever teach you how to cook?"

Pam turned to Sage, taking her eyes off the road for just a minute. She gave a light laugh. "What are you trying to say?"

Sage was relieved the question didn't upset her. "You never really cook meals like Nana's so I was just curious."

"Ma did teach me some tricks of the trade when I was younger, but we never made it a priority. Back when I was growing up, my parents stressed getting a good education. A lot of time was spent reading books and studying as opposed to hanging out in the kitchen. Looking back, it wouldn't have hurt to spend more time there." With that, Pam looked over at Sage and smiled. "Do you want to learn to cook like Nana?"

"I better if I want to keep smacking my lips, plus if I have a child one day I want to be able to feed her."

Pam gasped. "OK, now I'm offended. Don't I feed you?"

Sage laughed. "Ma, I didn't mean it that way. Yes, you feed me, but if I were to have a family years, years and many years from now, I want to put meals like Nana's on the table, you know?"

"Yeah I know—and your family will love you for it. When you get one, centuries and centuries from now."

They laughed together.

"Sorry baby."

"That's okay." Sage looked ahead to see that they were pulling into the apartment complex. It was small by Pam's standards. She'd been born in the Big Apple and New York had a way of making a lot of buildings and cities seem small, Pam always explained. She hadn't stayed in New York for long so she didn't 'claim' it much, but she talked about growing up and running around the asphalt jungle with buildings that seemed to touch the clouds.

Their complex was only three stories and the apartments opened up to the outside. To get to their apartment, they had to walk a flight of stairs. It was fine right now, but it could be a pain when they had a lot of groceries and it was especially hard on Nana sometimes.

As they got closer they noticed a few guys hanging around at the bottom of the stairs. Sage smiled at Aaron, the kid who lived in the apartment immediately above. He was a little older with a gentle soul.

They had a secret deal; she got the password to his protected wifi service so she didn't have to rely solely on her limited phone data, and she helped him with his history assignments when he got stuck. He looked at her and raised his chin up as she passed, his silent way of saying 'hey.' Sage followed her mom up the stairs. As soon as they got to the second flight, they began to smell Nana's cooking. Sage got even hungrier. She thought back to Sunday dinners before her Nana had moved in with them. Those had usually consisted of a can of Ravioli heated up with cheddar cheese sprinkled on the top, a cup of noodle soup, or Chinese Food—providing her mother decided to go all out. Sage didn't think any of those meals would fall across the five food groups, but didn't much have to worry about it anymore.

When they got into the apartment, Nana was sitting on the couch watching TV.

"Did you find what you needed baby?" Nana asked.

"Yes Nana," Sage said with a smile.

"Good, ya'll wash your hands and come on let's eat."

Sage walked back to her room to put the book away until later. The food smelled great—like chicken and something sweet—and she wanted to get back to the kitchen as quickly as possible so she could start throwin' down. She walked into the bathroom, grabbed the bar of soap and started washing her hands. Looking up into the mirror, Sage almost caught a glimpse of her mother. Never before had Sage thought she looked anything like her mother. She looked again, but lost the resemblance as quickly as she'd seen it.

Her mom was waiting as she came out of the bathroom. If Pam's two jobs ever got them a house, Sage had hoped it would have two bathrooms.

She'd stay in the bathroom for hours, just because she could.

Sage walked to the table and sat down. Pam came behind her about a minute later. Nana was moving about and fixing the plates and silverware. Sage and her mother often tried to place the plates or do other things in the kitchen, but that was Nana's domain and she didn't want them in there, "fiddlin' around." Once they all got seated, they held hands while Nana blessed the food and said grace. She thanked God for waking them up and letting them see another day, and for the meal on the table. She also asked him to say 'hi' to her baby, Patricia.

Patricia had been Pam's sister. Nana had a picture of her in a special box on her dresser. Sage never knew her aunt and neither had Sage's mom, for that matter. Sage was pretty sure she'd heard that Patricia was seven or eight years old when the family lost her to heaven. She'd been out playing and had run in the street after a ball or dog or something. Nana didn't talk much about what had happened to her. Sage did look at her aunt's picture on occasion. Patricia had been a taller version of her mother with caramel colored skin.

Nana was still saying Grace while Sage thought about her aunt, and last asked God to make clear to us all what gifts he gives so that we may use them for the betterment of his kingdom. Sage figured that was about the sixth time she'd heard the word gift today.

"Melanie called," her grandmother started after they'd gotten a few mouthfuls in. "She told me to tell you her parents were taking her to the church dinner and she wouldn't be able to come over."

Sage had her mouth full of food and nodded an OK. It wasn't a big surprise. Just about the only time Melanie had away from her parents was at school. In any case, she had ballet practice to get to. Sage had begun making her way through the chicken when her mother brought up the subject of the tryouts.

"Ma, did Sage tell you about her idea to perform ballet for the school talent show?"

Sage glanced at her mom, annoyed.

"Naw," Nana answered, turning to Sage. "Baby Girl, tell me about your idea."

"It's nothing. I just wanted to try something different—"

"Hmmm," Nana responded. "I didn't know you knew how to do ballet."

"I'm gonna do some exercises."

Pam sighed. "It just doesn't make any sense to me. You're heading for a fall, Sage."

"Well," Nana said, "if she wants to do somethin' she doesn't know anything about, so be it. She's the one that has to work through it and everything that comes with it."

Still her mother said, "I just don't know why Sage would do that to herself."

Sage put more chicken in her mouth, not trusting herself to speak. If Pam was going to talk like she wasn't even there, then she wouldn't waste time and energy defending her choice. After a long moment's quiet, Nana nudged Sage's hand.

"How's Melanie doing?"

Sage was grateful for the change of subject. "Okay, I guess. Why?"

"That girl needs to tame herself down, some. I seen her across the street acting up this last Friday." Nana shook her head solemnly. "There was a girl on her own and Melanie standing with a group of others, all pointing and whisperin'. That other lone girl looked like she was brinkin' on crying. I thought Melanie was bought up better than that."

"Melanie's picking up a lot of energy this year with no place to put it," Pam said.

"They gonna need to let that chile live a little or they gonna have a mess on their hands."

Sage shifted in her seat. She knew both her mom and Nana were right—since they entered seventh grade, Melanie's rebellious streak had gotten wider and wider. These days, Melanie seemed ready to sass just about anybody. Even Gina. Even *Lisa.* Sage shrugged at her Nana and chimed in. "I think she just feels stiffled and is looking for attention."

"Well, that's no good reason to be giving other people a hard time, is it?"

"Mom," Pam chipped in, "Sage is Melanie's friend, not her keeper."

"Just make sure your friendship don't go pulling you into any school wars," Nana warned Sage. "You and your Ma know it's not easy being an only-chile, but don't make too many excuses for your friend. Just give her a reminder or two when you can. It'll help her down life's road."

Sage noticed the strange look that passed between her mom and her Nana and decided she didn't want to be sitting up at the table anymore. She ate what was left of her meal and stood up. "That was delicious Nana, but I've got to go practice now."

Sage didn't always know how to take her Nana's advice. Sometimes she was great, getting Pam to back off when riding Sage a little hard about something, like the ballet. Other times, her Nana wouldn't give a yes-or-no comment on anything, or she'd be the voice of doom. As she walked to her room, Sage recalled her Nana's words about experimenting at the audition; *She's the one that has to work through it and everything that comes with it.*

Yeah, so she'd have to 'work through' impressing Darren Timberlake with her ballet skills, and becoming more popular after the tryouts. That didn't seem like a lot to deal with.

Sage changed into a pair of shorts and T-shirt and stood in front of her mirror to begin her stretches. She remembered how important that was. Once all loosened up, she reached over to the book lying on the bed and began to skim through the pages, looking at the positions. Close to the front, she found a position she remembered from when she took lessons. Sage stood up and looked in the mirror, trying to touch her heels together while pointing her toes outward. She bent and straightened without losing her balance.

About a half hour later, Sage's legs had begun to ache, and all she'd managed to do was strike each pose correctly. She was a long way from performing an actual dance. She watched about ten minutes of the ballet she'd recorded but everything she saw was so advanced. Sage sat down on the bed and began flipping through the book until she found information on Swan Lake. Maybe a really short segment from a famous dance would do. As she read more, she realized she had a lot to learn in two days. Every dance seemed to have a really complicated story behind it or require a partner.

Sage put her hand on her chin and wished she'd said she was going to do the two steps or one of the dances she would see on MTV. That would have been much easier to learn. Of course, that's not what would have stood out. Everyone and their mother would be doing their own take on the moves of those same dancers. She considered not being in the tryouts at all, but just couldn't give up the thought of seeing Darren Timberlake smiling up at her and, besides, she was just doing a short performance for the tryout, not trying to become a ballerina. All she needed was enough good moves to get her through Tuesday. She got a little more confidence and kept reading.

Sage's eyes were getting tired. She put the book down, rubbed her eyes then closed them for a few minutes. Her imagination got to work, putting her back on the school stage once again. This time, she was performing One, Two Step from Clara of the Nutcracker. She had her hair pulled into a bun on top like she'd seen ballerinas wear, and she could perform the moves perfectly. Everybody was going crazy and calling out her name. Sage began to fade off the stage into the dark. The darkness turned into sleep.

Chapter 4

Sage woke up to the gentle nudge of her grandmother.

"Come on baby, it's time for school."

She hadn't realized that she'd even fallen asleep. She'd only meant to sleep for a few minutes. The plan was to get up way early so she could practice on her ballet moves some more. Sage leaped out of bed, still in her shorts and T-shirt, frustrated that she'd wasted valuable time.

When she came out of the shower, she found her bed made up with a button down white shirt and khaki skirt lying on the cover. Her Nana always did this while she was in the shower, straightening up her bed and pulling out clothes she wanted to see Sage in for the day. Sometimes she just put on the clothes her Nana had chosen to make her feel good. If she liked the pants, but not the shirt, she'd put the outfit on but take a different shirt to school to change into. Today wasn't going to be one of those days.

The shirt was white with ruffles down the front, and Sage didn't feel like wearing a skirt today. Sage pulled out her white T-shirt and jeans. Nana wouldn't be mad; she and Nana had almost made a game out of Sage's decision to wear or not wear the selected clothes without either one ever saying anything. If Sage came out of the room in the clothes laid out, Nana would hug her tight, give her some change with a big kiss, and tell her how lady-like she looked.

Sage looked at her clock. She was running out of time. She brushed her hair back into a ponytail and put the ballet book into her bag along with her others in case she had a chance to look at it during one of her breaks at school. While she still had her bag open, she took a piece of paper and drew a happy face on it. She laid it on top of the rejected clothes.

Sage hurried through the front room and went to give Nana an exaggerated kiss. Nana looked over her glasses, checked out Sage's jeans and white tee, and handed her a jacket.

"Have a blessed day at school, Baby."

"Thank you, Nana," Sage said with a smile. If she'd worn what had been laid out, she might have gotten some spare change for school, but that didn't matter today. She'd missed out on seeing the happiness on Nana's face as she modeled the outfit of the day, but no doubt Nana would find a reason to go into her room today, and she'd see the note left for her.

Sage was close to the bus stop when she heard Melanie mouthing off at another student. As she turned the corner, she saw the girl Melanie was arguing with—a school mate by the name of Felecia. Sage groaned inside; no one in their right mind would mouth off at Felecia right now. Felecia's behavior had gotten more erratic over the summer and she was just returning from a suspension she'd received for skipping classes to hang out with some guys from school.

"...Don't nobody tell me what I can or cannot say," yelled Melanie, dipping her head from side to side.

"I know you better stop saying my name in a negative way when I don't want you saying it."

"How stupid is that? I can say your name however I want!"

"Hey! You two!" Sage interrupted.

Both of them looked over at her.

"What's up Sage," Felecia replied. "You need to chill this spoiled friend of yours before she gets hurt."

"Whose gonna hurt me?" Melanie said, standing back.

Sage smiled at Felecia, mouthed "sorry" and grabbed her friend by the arm; pulling her away.

"Hey girl," Melanie said, as if she hadn't been in the middle of a confrontation.

"Hey, are you trying to get Felecia to have a meltdown?"

"She's not going to do anything to me, let alone have a meltdown. She just got suspended so she can't mess up again."

Sage stopped and looked at Melanie. "What if Felecia doesn't care if she gets suspended again?"

Melanie looked over at Felecia, then back at Sage, suddenly troubled. "I hadn't thought about that."

Sage didn't have the energy. It was like Melanie's good sense had gone missing in action. They both turned at the sound of the bus coming down the other street. Sage nudged Melanie. "You better go grab your bag."

Melanie darted over to collect it from the middle of the sidewalk, where she'd left it. It was one of those bags that rolled, and Melanie scowled as she yanked it by the handle over to where Sage was standing. Sage couldn't blame Melanie for hating the bag. Pam had tried to encourage her to get one and she'd flat out refused. They were hard to maneuver in school, someone was always tripping over them, and they looked nerdy.

As the bus pulled over, Felecia strode right towards the doors, giving

Melanie's bag a good kick as she walked by. It flipped onto its side and the handle twisted out of Melanie's grip.

"What is wrong with you?" Melanie yelled, rubbing her wrist.

"You'll be asking yourself that question later on today." With that, Felecia stomped up the steps, shooting a dirty look over her shoulder.

Melanie turned her bag back on its wheels and they boarded the bus together, taking their usual seats right beside each other. Melanie was safe for now; no one bothered to act up on their bus. Their driver was serious and had been known to report each and every little violation to the bus monitor. They'd pulled off from school late on at least three occasions just because someone had gotten out of their seat for a second.

As the bus began to move, Sage turned to Melanie. "You're really pushing it. Felecia's not stable. What made you mouth off at her anyway?"

"I didn't really do anything."

Sage raised her brows and waited.

"She came to the bus stop and I just asked her what it was like being in suspension."

"Oh, Mel!"

"She gave me this...*look* and didn't say anything, so I just started calling her name. You know, Felecia. Felecia, answer me Felecia, boy-crazy Felecia—"

"Melanie, you're my friend and if you did that to me, I'd want to hurt you." Sage sighed.

Sage thought about Felecia. Anyone paying attention could see the changes in her this year. She'd always oscillated between being the center of a crowd, laughing with Eric Owens in tow and next being unusually quiet in class; sometimes asleep on the desk with teachers seeming to make exceptions letting her sleep. This school season, the laugher was louder; almost angry. The humor that had attracted most people to her had been replaced with sarcasm.

"Well, I don't think she's going to hurt me. She's just blowin' smoke. Anyway, what did you end up doing after I called? I called back, but you'd already left for the mall."

Sage reached into her book bag and pulled out her book on ballet. "I got this book so I could freshen up on some ballet moves before the tryouts."

"Are you still planning to go through with that?"

Sage ignored the eye-roll. "I already have a few good moves down now, and I'll have more before the auditions tomorrow. Are you singing for sure?"

"Yep, I have an idea. Why don't you play your sax and I sing? We'd make a great duo?"

"I can play the sax for you if you need me to, but I really want to show—" Sage cleared her throat, remembering Melanie had been there when she was trying to impress Darren. "I want to show myself that I can do this."

Her friend looked over at her with a smirk on her face. Sage was not fooling her. Melanie took the book from Sage and began thumbing through the pages.

Sage looked out the bus window and thought about auditions. This time, Darren's aunt wasn't there but he was, helping out behind the curtains and watching the performance before Sage's. She walked up behind him, still doing her stretches.

She stopped by him and held onto her foot from the back, stretching her leg way up behind.

"Oh, hey…" he said, staring, impressed with her flexibility. Of course he'd know that very few people could do this move. Some Olympic figure skaters mastered the pose, but that was about it. He shuffled from foot to foot. "What music do you have to start this one off?"

"The Party Scene from The Nutcracker," she replied with a smile.

"Wow. I can't wait to see you perform. I told my aunt that we had someone in the school that did ballet, and she wants to meet you the next time she comes into town. I'll invite you over to the house."

"I would love to meet your—huh?" Sage blinked as Melanie's hand waved up and down in front of her face. She took the book that Melanie was trying to pass back to her..

"What were you looking at?"

"Nothin'. I was just looking out at the street."

Melanie snorted.

When the bus got to the school, Melanie and Sage went their separate ways. Sage got to her home room class where she dropped her books off, then headed to the cafeteria to eat breakfast. She was never very hungry in the mornings, but a lot of students ate there instead of at home and it was a way to sit around and chat before the day began. Because students weren't allowed to stay in the cafeteria unless they were eating something, Sage picked up a box of cereal. She looked around and not seeing any of her friends, noticed Foster, seated alone.

"Mind if I sit here."

Foster looked up, then to both sides as if someone else was around.

Sage took that as an invitation and sat down.

Darren walked into the cafeteria with another student Sage didn't know. She tried not to watch them too obviously as they walked over to the line to pick up their food. Sage turned back towards Foster, hoping he hadn't caught on that she had been staring at Darren.

Sage poured the Raisin Brand into the plastic bowl and while pouring the milk, looked up at Foster.

Foster was looking right at her with a nervous look.

"How are you today, Foster."

"Fine, better today."

"Better than what," Sage responded with an outward chuckle.

"Well, not as sick."

Sage really looked at him this time. Putting a spoon of cereal in her mouth and chewing, she felt awkward.

Sick from what, she thought.

She looked at him and smiled realizing how beautiful his blue, green eyes were. Foster was so frail, she'd spent more time feeling bad for him, then looking at him.

"Did you have a cold," Sage added while scooping up another spoonful.

He snorted, "I wish."

He remained quiet for a few seconds, then added, "Cancer."

"Cancer?" That's pretty serious isn't it?

"Yea, it's pretty serious," he chuckled.

Sage began asking questions and he relaxed, taking some comfort in her innocence. He answered her questions; sharing how he'd been on heavier drugs that made him nauseous and lose weight, but had begun a new treatment this year with less side effects; plus he was going into remission. As she listened, she realized he was no one to feel sorry for.

Sage continued to listen while eating the cereal, barely tasting it while engrossed in Foster's story.

Foster finished his breakfast and as much as he was going to share and asked if it was ok for him to go to class; as if Sage were a teacher.

Sage smiled and said, "see you later Foster." It was almost time to leave and the bell would ring soon, she got up to throw her plastic bowl in the trash can.

"Ballerina!"

Sage turned at the sound of Darren's voice and almost turning to jello at the smile on his face. She moved to wave at him, but he was already turning to wander off with his friend. She was so flustered that she sped up her walk and almost ran out of the cafeteria, Her encounter jolting her back to her new found reality. Both embarrassed and excited at the same time. She'd just known that her doing ballet would impress people and make her popular! Already she had a cute nickname, with Darren of all people calling it out in the cafeteria. Now she was determined to make this work! Sage rushed to her homeroom class. She was going to study at every break and every minute when she got home after school.

When Sage got home, Nana had a sandwich for her to eat.

"Oh…thanks!" She took the plate and hustled towards her room.

"You not going to eat that out here with me? Tell me about school today?"

Sage grimaced, feeling a little guilty. "I'm sorry Nana, but I've got to practice."

"Ok baby girl…" Nana shuffled over and kissed her on the cheek.

Sage spent the rest of the evening learning her moves and felt pretty good about what she'd accomplished until she realized she didn't have any good music to go with it. She didn't want anything too classical, but the music she had in her room was too raw. Nobody wanted to see a Swan Dance performed to "My Goodies."

Sage found the tape recorder her mom had bought her years ago, got out her third-hand, first-generation iPad, and then took her sax from her case. Over the next couple of hours, she thought through her routine, the beat she needed to dance to, and where the crescendos in the music needed to be. Since most of her moves would be slow and smooth, she figured that she could get the mellow sounds and volume she needed from her sax, if she could just find the right underlay tunes. Her GarageBand app proved amazing to help pull together the whole sound and she recorded her sax overlay take in one go, on both iPad and cassette. Sage sent quiet prayers of thanks to Aaron for use of his wifi signal as she stored her new dancing score in the cloud.

Once finished, she began the moves to her Swan Dance, following the rhythm of her new backing tune.

Great. This'll work!

A knock sounded at the door. Sage opened up to see her Nana standing there, and for a moment she thought she was in trouble for staying up so late. Then she realized Nana was smiling.

"Hey Baby, I don't mean to bother you, but that's a beautiful song you playin' there. What is the name of it?"

"Oh, I don't have one, Nana. I just made it up for the dance I'm going to do tomorrow."

"You mean you just… made that tune up like that? I knew you were talented, but Lor' chile, that's nothin' but a gift from God."

Sage kept her smile in place. *Not this 'gift' thing, again!* "Thank you Nana, but I got to finish practicing—"

"Why didn't you want to make up some music for the talent show?"

"Because, Nana. Just because."

"You sure could do a lot with that music, like play in the church band or somethin'!"

"You can have it after I finish, okay?"

Sage felt bad about pushing her Nana out the door, but she had to get back to what she was doing. She didn't have any time to waste.

Chapter 5

It was Sage's turn.

She limped over to the music deck, where Ms. Whitaker had set up a laptop, a cassette-player and a whole stack of amps. Sage slotted her CD into the laptop. Her shoulder hurt just moving the mouse around the table and she couldn't help her hands trembling with nerves.

She'd been like this all day, her muscles hurting terribly, from the moment she'd sat down at one of the consoles in the computer room to see if she could download her music from the cloud. She couldn't figure out how to get anything to work and was ready to scream when Eric Miller came in and helped her out. He got her music burned to a CD and even wrote on the case inlay for her. "Darren tells me you're doing ballet," he'd said with an ear-to-ear grin. "Good for you. A guy can only sit through so many songs by Beyonce wannabes."

She'd given him a weak smile and awkward hug of gratitude before taking her CD and walking out, super-slowly, pretending she couldn't hear him when he asked if she'd hurt herself.

Yeah, she'd *really* hurt herself.

Sage forced her legs up the little steps that led up the back of the stage. She hadn't realized that pushing herself to learn the ballet would make her so sore. She hoped she didn't look as bad as she felt.

At least she'd recorded fifteen seconds of silence ahead of her music to give her time to get into position. Once on stage, she looked out to the audience, which was filled with students waiting their turn and a few teachers. Darren had been in the audience earlier, but now Sage didn't see him. She'd been trying to spot him during the last performance, but he seemed to have disappeared. If he didn't show up in the next minute, all this would be for nothing. She looked around one last time to see if Darren had come back in, but then the first long note of her sax filled the room, pumping out from the speakers over the soft drum bass she'd laid down on the recording.

She couldn't see much because of the bright lights in her eyes, but thought she saw a few feet tapping in the front row of the audience.

Feeling a little more confident, she talked herself through every move, trying to keep time.

Stretch arms outward, bring them down and now leg out slowly...

She did the spins and jumps like the pictures showed, but her thighs hurt so badly she almost felt like she couldn't get up high enough and her landings felt heavy. She didn't fall or stagger though and got through to her final spins before lying on the floor with her legs crossed. The music stopped and Sage stood up.

The silence was total, to start with. It filled slowly with the sounds of feet shuffling and chairs scraping across the floor.

Sage looked out to the audience for smiles and nodding heads, but as the hall lights came up, all she could see was a sea of blank looks. There seemed to be so many people out there, all of a sudden. And none of them were clapping.

"Thank you, Sage," Ms. Whitaker said, scribbling on her clipboard. "Can we have Jack and Riley up here, please?"

Sage hobbled off the stage, took her CD tape out of the recording unit and walked over to her sweats. There were students standing behind the curtain, but they didn't say anything about her performance. She started feeling weird, like she was numb in all the places she'd been achy just moments ago. And she was shaking. She saw Melanie sitting way at the back of the audience and walked down to her aisle, sliding in beside her.

Melanie dropped her face down into her hands. "Girl, I don't know what you were thinking."

"Was it *that* bad?"

"Did you hear anybody clap?"

"N-no." Sage felt like she'd been punched in the stomach. She folded her arms. All that work for nothing. She could feel her eyes welling up. She wanted to get up and leave right then, but didn't want to bring any more attention to herself. She looked around the audience for Darren and finally spotted him coming in through the back doors. That just made her angrier. She felt so stupid. Not only had she embarrassed herself in front of all those people, but the one person she'd done all that work for hadn't even seen her perform.

She lifted her arms up to her eyes and pretended to stretch so nobody would see how hard she was trying not to cry. People were muttering to each other in the audience and some girls were looking back at her, sniggering. She pressed her forearm to her eyes to apply pressure. This was just…horrible. She wiped her face dry, taking consolation in one thing—at least Darren had not been there to see her crash and burn. Though probably he'd hear the gossip that she'd really sucked.

Sage sniffed and sat up straight.

Melanie's parents were giving them a ride home so she had to wait until Melanie finished and they showed up. Her heart sank as Jack and Riley left the stage to the sounds of huge applause and she sat through the rest of the auditions with her arms folded across her chest. Most of the students that tried out were okay, and some of them not so good. Sage couldn't help but feel as sorry for the bad ones as she was feeling for herself.

Melanie was one of the last up and sang "I'm still Jenny from the block" by J-Lo. Sage knew Melanie's parents hadn't yet arrived by the way Melanie was shakin' it up on that stage. If they'd been around, she would have been standing there like a statue. Her voice was good though, and people liked to hear it whatever she sang.

Finally it was time to leave and Sage couldn't have been happier. Ms. Whitaker thanked everyone for their participation and hard work and announced that everyone would find out whether or not they'd made the show by tomorrow afternoon. The posting would be listed in the main office so they could check there.

Sage joined Melanie at the back of the auditorium where her parents were now waiting.

"How were tryouts?' Melanie's mother asked.

Sage smiled and let out a "fine."

Excited about her performance, Melanie walked alongside her parents talking a mile a minute while Sage dragged her feet behind them. Sage watched as the three of them went ahead. It was always the three of them. Sage realized that in all the time she'd known the James family, she'd never seen Mr. and Mrs. James apart from one another. As quickly as the thought crossed her mind, it left and she began to think of how poorly she had done. They all reached the car and Sage climbed into the back seat beside Melanie, who seemed like she needed to hear how good she was over and over again.

"Are you sure I was okay?" she asked for the fourth time.

"Yeah, you were good." Sage hadn't asked Melanie about how she'd looked since coming off the stage. At first she didn't want to hear any more of Melanie's honest opinions, but now she just wanted to change the topic from her friend's awesomeness.

"Was my dance as bad as you made it sound when I came off the stage?"

"It was horrible," Melanie said "I felt so bad for you. You looked like an arthritis patient trying to do an aerobic exercise or something."

Sage couldn't help but laugh at the analogy. If the comment had come from anyone else, she probably would have been ready to cry all over again.

"My muscles were so sore from practicing that I couldn't move all that well."

"Is that what that was? I wondered why you were moving so slow. Anyway, it was bad."

"I know." Sage gritted the word out while faking a smile.

"That song you had was the bomb though. Where did you buy that CD?"

"I just made that up last night so I could have something to play."

"What?"

"Yeah, I realized at the last minute that I didn't have anything else so

I made something up real quick."

"*Say what*?!" Melanie sat there with her mouth wide open again.

Sage couldn't understand why Melanie always did that. She felt like throwing something in there just to make sure Melanie didn't do it anymore.

Melanie finally got a grip and said, "Where's the CD?"

"In my bag."

"Get it out."

Sage reached into the bag and got out the case. She handed it to Melanie.

"Daddy, can you put this into the player?"

"Sure." Melanie's father reached back, opened the case and slotted the disc in.

Sage had put the music together only for the purpose of the Swan Dance and hadn't paid that much attention to anything other than getting it finished in time, but as she listened to it play, she realized that it was beautiful. The melodies rose and fell with soft and then strong crescendos. It seemed like a combination of jazz and classical, bold but fun at the same time. As Sage listened her mind began to wander as it so often did, but this time not in a day dream. This time, she thought of her Nana's face as she'd stood at the door of her bedroom asking her the name of the song. She thought of her Nana's prayers and her mother's words, and even the Pastor's intense sermon came back in a flash. How could she not appreciate her own talent and gift from God?

Melanie's father voice broke into Sage's thoughts. "I can't believe you composed this song in one day."

"Yes sir, I did." Sage said, keeping it to herself that she'd composed it in a few hours.

Melanie's mother finally spoke a few long moments after the song finished. "Sage, I've known you since you were a baby and didn't know you were so talented. That is absolutely beautiful."

"Thank you," was all Sage could come up with. She felt herself blush. She looked over to Melanie, who was smirking, but not nastily. Sage was just happy to see her mouth closed.

"You should have played that song for the talent show."

"Oh, change the record!" Sage laughed along with Melanie, but she knew her friend was right. She looked out the window of the car, wishing that for once in her life she'd listened.

Chapter 6

Sage was playing her saxophone. It was dark in the room she played in. No one was around to hear, but for once that was OK. Sage played her heart out. Slowly a light started to come on and Sage put her instrument down. She heard her Nana's voice in the background.

"Come on, get up for school Baby," her Nana said.

Sage sat up in the bed and grunted. It would be nice if some of her best sax-playing took place during the daytime, not just in her dreams. But then…her Nana liked what she'd played in the evening two nights back. And the Jameses had really liked her recording…

"Nana," Sage called, as Nana began walking out of the door.

"Yes, baby?"

"Thank you for asking about my song the other night."

Nana stood in the hallway. "You're welcome baby. It sounded so pretty."

Sage's Nana came back into the room and sat on the bed with Sage. Her eyes had begun to water.

Sage didn't realize the song would mean so much to her Nana. "Are you all right?"

Her Nana let out a sigh. "I know I don't talk much about your auntie Patricia and your mama never knew her, but Pat was talented in music like you. Lord, that girl could pick up any instrument and play anything she wanted. Pat liked to hear herself play too."

Sage watched her Nana as she chuckled to herself.

"She couldn't get enough of playing stuff. We didn't have much money so it was hard to buy her an instrument. She would play up somethin' at the church though and we all loved to hear her. She'd be up at the crack of dawn on Sunday so she could get into that church and bang on something." Nana stopped to giggle at that thought and Sage was happy to see the memory made her Nana happy. Nana went on. "Your grandpa worked extra jobs to get up some extra money to buy her an instrument and finally one day brought home a fine clarinet, God rest his soul."

Sage smiled. "Did she love it?"

Nana slapped her knee. "Lor' chile, Pat was so excited. She played that thing every day for the last few days of her life. We lost her two weeks after she got that clarinet. I always figured that her music was so perfect, God decided he wanted her right beside him playin' for him and those angels."

Sage's Nana went quiet and deep in thought. Her eyes looked like they were far away. Finally, she seemed to come back. She looked up with a wet smile and patted Sage's hand.

With that, her Nana got up and walked out of the room.

Sage was stunned. All that time, her talent had reminded Nana of her own daughter's, but Nana had never said anything. Sage couldn't figure why. Maybe she had felt it would be too much pressure? Or maybe it just hurt too much to think about it.

Sage couldn't get the story Nana had told out of her mind while she showered and did her teeth. She recalled the picture she'd seen in Nana's room. Her aunt looked so happy and to know a little more about her made

Sage begin to smile. She *needed* to smile. The idea of going into school today with everyone talking about her ballet performance made her gut run cold. Still, Sage now knew that her Nana was right more often than she'd given her credit for. After that awful performance, Sage now had to work through "everything that came with it." She sighed. Unfortunately, this included braving it out at school.

Sage left the bathroom and went into her room. True to form, Nana had picked out some clothes for Sage to wear. This time, Nana had picked the khaki skirt with a navy blue turtle neck sweater. She'd gone so far as to pull out some tights and shoes. Sage smiled and put the outfit on. When she looked in the mirror, she figured Nana had done good today.

Sage retrieved the CD from her bag, got all the rest of her things together and walked into the kitchen, where Nana sat with her glasses. Nana looked up and smiled hard.

"You look like such a lady today, Sage. Here's some change for you. I want you to have a blessed day."

Sage hugged and kissed her Nana, but didn't take the change. Instead she placed the CD into her Nana's hands. "You have a blessed day too, Nana. This will play in mom's CD player, by her bed. I'll see you when I get home.

Sage's Nana looked the happiest Sage had ever seen her. She clutched the CD to her heart and rubbed Sage's back as she walked out the door of the apartment.

Sage walked to the bus stop and found she was a little early today. Only she and one other student were waiting. Melanie hadn't taken the bus to school yesterday and they'd had a lift home, so Felecia's threat still hung in the air. As Sage saw Melanie dragging her book bag down the street, she hoped Felecia had forgotten about Melanie mouthing off at her and calling her boy crazy. Melanie got to the bus stop.

"Hey, Sage. I wonder if Felecia's going to catch the bus today?"

"I don't know," Sage answered. She could tell Melanie was nervous, but who wouldn't be? The only thing that was working in her favor was that Felecia was a chronic absentee. She was always missing the bus and, just as often, the full day of school. They stood there for a while with Melanie looking down the street every couple of seconds, too agitated to talk much. After a while, most of the students that caught the bus were at the stop. The bus approached and Sage could tell Melanie had begun to relax a little.

But then they looked back down the street and saw Felecia approaching from the other direction. She'd make it—she was walking pretty fast. Sage and Melanie both got closer to the street, poised to jump on board as soon as the doors opened.

Felecia, catching up behind them, pushed against Melanie. "*You* got lucky today."

Melanie turned around and looked Felecia up and down. "Oh no. You got lucky today."

As the bus doors opened, Sage let Melanie walk up the steps in front of her. They got to their seat and sat down.

Sage started in on a lecture that seemed all too familiar. "Girl, what are you thinking?"

"I can't act like I'm scared of her!"

"Why not? Aren't you?"

"If I act like I'm scared of her, she's just going to keep on pickin' on me."

Sage threw her head back in amazement. She could never figure her friend out. "She wasn't pickin' on you to begin with! You are tossing gasoline on a small fire!"

Melanie just sat there, looking up at the front of the bus where Felecia sat. She didn't answer. Sage had known Melanie long enough to know that meant she agreed, but wasn't about to admit it. Melanie started to talk about the talent show and her performance again. Sage just listened. She was concerned for her friend, but was at a lost on how to help her from getting herself hurt. Melanie spent so much time trying to gain freedom by being tough and sassy as if being both would break her chains. Sage nodded in all the right places as Melanie talked about what she would probably wear for the talent show, going through her entire wardrobe and a host of other outfits in her mind.

'I'm thinking a orange halter and some jeans, or maybe some shorts with a large waist length sweat top might work. Which one of those do you think would look best?"

"Orange halter and jeans" Sage replied, knowing all too well that Melanie's parents would probably not let her wear a third of the outfits she kept talking about.

"How should I wear my hair?" Melanie asked excitedly.

Sage looked down. Melanie's hair was shoulder length and healthy. She usually wore it curled under in a bob-type style. "You could wear it up with it falling out like a waterfall on top," Sage said, demonstrating the look with her hands.

Melanie put her hands through her hair and pushed it up to get a feel for it working or not. "Hum, might work."

Sage pretended to listen to Melanie talk the rest of the way to school, but her mind had begun to wander and before long she was in a day dream once again.

She'd made it to the talent show and felt all the excitement Melanie was feeling as she scrambled around getting her outfit together and making up a beautiful song to play. At last, she chose to wear a long skirt with boots, a white T and a denim jacket that stopped right at the waist. Her mother had a tan hat Sage always loved and she'd let Sage wear it for the show. It was Sage's turn to go on and she went to the middle of the stage. The audience was dead silent. Sage looked down at the audience, seeing her Nana and mother sitting in the second row, and put her sax up to her mouth. Sage closed her eyes and could feel the music in her head. If she wanted to change a note mid-stream, she could. She played and played because it felt like a part of her and for once, it made her feel good. Sage came to the end of her song she looked up. The audience was still dead silent.

"I'll catch up with you during lunch," Melanie said.

Sage came out of her daydream and picked up her bags. They had arrived at school. Time to face yesterday's mess.

Chapter 7

Sage had begun to feel miserable as she walked to her class. Not only had she missed out on performing at the talent show, but now, as she got closer to her homeroom, she was reminded of how bad she must have looked on stage the night before.

She walked past some students she had seen at her tryout on her way to the cafeteria reaching up to rub her neck. They were leaning against the wall of one of the buildings, looking over at her. As she got a little closer, she heard one of them make comments about ballerina wanna-bes, making sure they were loud enough for her to hear.

Sage decided to skip breakfast and headed for her home room, clutching her books tight to her chest. She kept her head down, resting her chin on them. The other day, the nickname *Ballerina* had seemed so important. Now it was being used to mock her. She was so deep in thought, she almost ran into Ms. Whitaker as she turned the corner.

"Whoa!" said Ms. Whitaker as they almost collided.

"I'm sorry" said Sage, reaching down to pick up the counselor's pad.

"How are you this morning, Sage?" she asked with a chirpy smile.

"Fine."

Ms. Whitaker stood there smiling and clearly waiting for another response, but Sage just twisted up her face in a half way smile and moved around her so she could make it to class.

"Sage?"

"Yes?"

"I meant to ask you the name of that song you played last night during your tryout."

"I didn't name it yet. I gave it to my grandmother."

"I don't quite understand."

"I didn't name the song when I wrote it."

Ms. Whitaker stood there surprised. So surprised, she looked like Melanie with her mouth open. "Sage, you can write music like that? Who played the instrument?"

"I did. I wrote it and played it with my sax."

Ms. Whitaker's eyes seemed to double their size. "Why didn't you play your instrument and that song for the tryouts?"

Sage stood there and shrugged her shoulders. She felt bad enough about her decision—she didn't even want to explain it at this point.

"Look, uh…" Ms. Whitaker looked around as if she was looking for someone to help her think what to say next. "I can talk to the judges to see if they'll let you play your instrument and music in the talent show. After all, you did play it during the tryouts. Maybe you can open up for the show or end it. What do you think about that?"

Sage perked up. "Okay…" was all she could think of to say, but the smile on her face felt much more real than the ones she'd been dishin' out earlier.

"I can't promise anything, but I'll let you know what I find out by the end of today."

"Thank you," Sage responded and walked towards class in a daze.

She was shocked at how good she felt after being so low, before. Now she might be able to perform after all, and maybe people would forget about her stupid, stupid dance. If she couldn't compete, at least she would be able to open or close—providing the judges agreed.

Sage literally skipped to her homeroom and turning one corner almost knocked Foster down.

"Oh sorry and hey … she laughed. Are you feeling ok today Foster?"

"Yea" with a shy giggle. Foster responded.

"Sure?" Sage repeated with a raised brow, now knowing more about him.

He looked straight at her; clearly moved. "Sure." He responded with a wink and a smile.

"Great! Sorry again," she smiled and skipped off to class.

Sage arrived to class early, picked up her pencil and some paper and began scratching some tunes she could use in a new song. If she did get the chance to perform in the talent show, she'd make sure she did her best. She thought about Darren Timberlake and what he would think of her talent and for some reason… it just didn't seem important anymore. She wanted to do this for herself. No one else seemed to matter at this point.

* * * *

Sage's good mood began to die down as the school day came to an end. She still hadn't heard from Ms. Whitaker. She'd gone through each class waiting for Ms. Whitaker to stick her head in the door, or for the intercom to call her name to the counselor's office, but none of that happened.

The only good thing was that she'd come up with some possible names for her new song. It had been a long time since Sage even paid much attention to her music.

She was rounding the corner to her civics class when she saw Melanie laughing with some friends.

Melanie ran towards her, looking over-excited. "We MADE it!" she said, hugging Sage tight. "We made it into the talent show."

Sage was happy for her, smiling both at Melanie and her friends. "I knew you would. You sounded really good up there."

"Yeah, I know, but 'we' includes you! Your name's on the list."

"What?" She'd deliberately avoided it on purpose. Since Ms. Whitaker hadn't come back to her, she'd decided she couldn't bear the disappointment a second time.

"I guess that ballet routine worked after all."

Sage rolled her eyes but couldn't resist Melanie's teasing wink or cheeky grin. She was too happy to be mad and told Melanie about her discussion with Ms. Whitaker.

"That makes sense. You're going to be the bomb." Melanie grabbed a hug from her friend again. "I'm so glad we're going to be in it together."

"Me too," Sage said. At that moment, Sage heard her name called from behind her. She turned around and saw Ms. Whitaker striding in her direction as Melanie ran off to her last class.

"Hi Sage," Ms. Whitaker said, out of breath, "I couldn't get to you earlier—"

"It's fine. I just found out from Melanie that I was on the list. Thank you *so* much, Ms. Whitaker."

"All right, then. Good luck with your performance. I'm sure you'll do beautifully." With that, Ms. Whitaker walked off and Sage went into her class.

Civics was one of her least favorite subjects. The teacher was fun, but the subject didn't keep her interested. She sat down at her desk. The teacher began to talk about the Executive and Legislative branches of government. It only took Sage a few moments to transplant her mind from the class room to church, where she was playing her saxophone.

She was one of two young people playing in the church band. Most everybody else was old or older, as her mom liked to say. She was playing a solo and everyone was swaying to the music. She almost wanted to climb into the music herself. While she played, she felt her aunt Patricia by her side playing the clarinet. They sounded as if they'd been practicing together forever. No one seemed to want to stop them and they didn't care to stop so they kept on playing.

"Sage, do you know the answer?"

Sage came back to class. "Huh?"

"Well, what about the question is difficult?"

Sage sat there, embarrassed. She could tell her civics teacher wasn't about to let her off the hook. She just stood there, looking at Sage for an answer. Sage's cheeks flushed. "I'm sorry but I missed the question."

"What legislative powers does the Executive branch have over the Legislative branch?"

Sage thought for a second. "They… call Congress into special session and can veto?"

"Correct. Sage, just pay attention so I don't have to repeat myself. You're distracting the class."

"Yes. Sorry."

Sage paid attention for the remainder of the class, but could hardly wait to get home and tell her Nana and mother she made the talent show with her music. All of a sudden the name of the song came to her— *Patricia*. She'd see what her Nana thought, first.

Chapter 8

Melanie was trembling when Sage slid into her seat next to her on the bus home. Sage took one quick look at Felecia, who was laughing loudly, almost manic-like, while looking over at them. She held back a sigh as Melanie looked up at her with eyes like saucers.

"Sage, Felecia saw me in school today and didn't look right. You've got to walk me to my house. She's making me nervous."

"I'll walk you to your house, but I don't see how that's going to stop her from bothering you."

"She won't jump on both of us if she knows you're there."

"Melanie…" Sage picked her words carefully. "I'll walk with you, but you may want to apologize too."

"Apologize?!"

Sage shook her head, trying not to be hurt at the way Melanie was demanding things and snapping at her. It wasn't like Melanie ever felt she had to watch her tone. Although things had worked out fine with the talent contest, Melanie's harsh reaction to her dancing still rankled a little. Sage jumped as Melanie elbowed her in the side.

"Ow!"

"If you don't help me, why would I consider you a friend?"

"Why would you ask your friend to get hurt over something you did wrong and why would you question our friendship with everything I put up with?"

Their raised voices made some students look at them. They had to have been loud to have been heard over the sounds of everyone else talking and the loud motor of the bus. Sage scowled, folded her arms and stared out of the window, away from Melanie. She'd spent a lot of time over the last few months explaining Melanie's moods to people and apologizing for her so Melanie didn't lose too many friends. Sage felt she'd been totally loyal, but it seemed that the only loyalty that mattered to Melanie was that she was ready to hit Felecia for her.

Felecia sat near the front of the bus and continued to look back each time the bus stopped to let students off.

Neither Sage nor Melanie spoke for the remainder of the ride home. Once off the bus, they spent a few moments staying still on the sidewalk to let Felecia get a little ways down the street before following her towards Melanie's home, which was in the same direction. Five or so other students got off the bus with them, all going the same way.

Even though Sage was upset with Melanie, she did stay close beside her as they walked towards her home.

Sage knew trouble was about to brew when the bus pulled off. Felecia turned back to see it go out of sight and then stopped where she was standing.

Melanie moved a little closer to Sage.

"Since you like callin' my name so much, why don't you call it now?" Felecia yelled.

Melanie froze, her knuckles going tense around the handle of her book bag. Sage saw all the other students start to look up from their phones and look in their direction.

"I don't hear you sayin' nothin' now. You was all mouth the other mornin' talkin' 'bout some Felecia, Felecia, Felecia. What happened? You don't like my name no more?!"

Sage had frozen alongside Melanie while listening to Felecia practically screaming. Melanie gave her a look of total panic and took a few steps back, dragging her book bag off its wheels for a moment and scraping it across the sidewalk. Felecia had begun to walk fast towards them. All of a sudden Melanie took off running, her book bag still dragging behind her, its wheels banging and bashing against the ground.

Felecia was now close, ready to run around or through Sage to get to Melanie.

"Wait, Felecia. Wait!" Sage put her hands out to stop her, barely grabbing Felecia's arm as she rushed past. "Wait Felecia, she didn't mean it!"

"Let me go!" Felecia swung at Sage, almost hitting her in the face. She snatched her arm out of Sage's grasp and went running after Melanie.

Sage's attempt to stop Felecia had only afforded Melanie a little running room. She was still struggling to get away, hauling the book bag behind her. Running alongside were the other students who'd gotten off the bus, trying to keep up so they wouldn't miss any of the excitement.

"Melanie! Drop the bag!" Sage yelled out, but Melanie didn't. Sage gritted her teeth and sprinted after Melanie, Felecia and all the other students. If Melanie had just let the thing go, she'd probably been able to avoid what happened next.

Felecia caught up to Melanie, grabbing her collar and yanking her back. As Melanie fell, Felecia kicked the book bag, sending both the bag and Melanie flying, her wrist all caught up in the handle. Felecia began hitting on Melanie while the other students crowded round, using their phones to record the fight. They didn't even seem to care who won. Melanie was trying to shield herself, putting her hands up where Felecia kept swinging. Sage lurched over and grabbed Felecia's arm again, but this time Felecia snatched back and actually hit Sage. Sage wasn't one to fight, but the hit hurt! She swung back, hitting Felecia in the chest and face.

Finally, one other student stepped in to try and stop Felecia from hitting Sage back, but that only seemed to give her more reason to keep swinging. Melanie was trying to stand up, but Felecia broke free, poised to start hitting again.

"Hey!"

An elderly man finally came out of his house, screaming at them to stop fighting. Sage looked as the man, fit and fast for someone with grey hair, start to jog toward them. Felecia threw one last hit at Melanie's head, then she turned and ran away.

Melanie was on the ground, her arms covering her head.

Sage reached her hand out to Melanie to pull her up. "Are you okay?"

Melanie didn't respond. Instead, she pulled her arms from her head and looked past Sage in an effort to locate Felecia. Once she'd seen her nemesis halfway down the street, walking fast, Melanie stood up slowly.

The elderly man pushed through the crowd of students, getting to Melanie. "Whoa. Are you okay?"

"Y-y-yeah." replied Melanie.

"You sure? You have quite a bit of blood on you," the adult pointed out. "You wanna come in? Get washed up? I have band aids?"

Sage followed the man's gaze to Melanie, who'd finally looked down at her hands and noticed the blood from her grazes. She then looked down at her knees and noticed they were scraped and bloody, too. Her eyes started to tear up.

"Where do you live, young lady?"

"Not far," Melanie said, now in tears.

Sage had picked up Melanie's bookbag.

The grownup looked concerned, but didn't say anything else. Sage met his gaze and mouthed *it's all right.*

Melanie took her book bag from Sage and started to walk home.

Sage turned to the other students, thanking the one and asking the others to delete the recording. After much persuasion, they seemed to agree. She then jogged to catch up to Melanie.

"She didn't even hurt me," Melanie said out of the blue, sniffling and crying the whole time.

Sage didn't respond. She knew Melanie was hurt and even if she said she wasn't, Sage was hurt for her. Melanie's ego had to be as bruised as her body, the way Felecia beat on her, let alone it being captured on video. They reached Melanie's house and Sage waved her off, watching her walk up to her porch with her hair a little out of place and her skirt with dirt and blood spots all over it.

As Sage walked home, she dreaded what would happen next. Melanie would be the petite victim who got beat up by the mean and bad girl, Felecia. No one would even question her side of the story, since her parents were church-going pillars of the community. Melanie's parents would hear the story and call Pam to get her support. From there, they'd march down to Felecia's house, demanding justice for Felecia having put her hands on Melanie.

And the whole thing would be pointless. From what Sage had heard, Felecia's parents were just as out of it as she was. The James' would achieve nothing except to make Felecia's parents mad for something that Melanie had started, and Sage would probably be expected to take Melanie's side on everything.

Sage dragged her feet along the sidewalk. The further away she got from Melanie's house, the more she realized she might not be able to give a hundred percent support this time. Melanie had provoked the beating. Sure, while it was never good to hit people, everyone seemed to forget you could hit just as hard with words as you could a hand. And Melanie had never shown a moment of regret for how mean she'd been to Felecia in the first place.

Sage had always stood behind Melanie and always would, but there was a limit to what she could do for her. Sage couldn't help but hold her friend somewhat responsible for badgering Felecia the way she did. As Sage got closer to the apartment, she tried putting Melanie's situation out of her mind. She couldn't do anything about it until the next day anyway, and she wanted to enjoy telling her good news to Nana. She picked up the pace and got back to her apartment in just a few minutes.

When she opened the door, there sat Nana in the living room, watching the stories.

"Hey, Baby."

"Hi Nana," replied Sage with a big smile.

"Oh, oh, why you got that big smile on your face for? Somethin' good musta happened."

"It did! I made the talent show," Sage blurted out.

"What, you really could do that ballerina stuff, huh?"

Sage laughed at this. "No Nana, I couldn't do that ballerina stuff that good. As a matter of fact, I was terrible. You know that song I made up and gave to you? Well, that's the music I used for my dance, and Ms. Whitaker really liked it. She got me put in the show."

Sage was grinning from ear to ear. Her Nana slapped her knee in laughter.

"Baby, that's great you got into that show like you wanted. I'm so happy for you."

Sage hugged her grandma again. "Thanks, Nana."

Right then, they heard a key in the door. The door opened and Sage's mother came in, looking cheerful.

"The power went out at work," she announced. "They couldn't get it back on so they let us out early. Believe me when I say I'm not complaining!" Pam stopped and glanced between her mom and Sage. "Why are you two glowing like that?"

"I made the talent show," Sage said with a smile, and was almost shocked when Pam shot forward and squeezed her with a huge hug. It took a few moments to explain everything, but she had her mom's undivided attention while Nana bustled around making sandwiches. Sage felt so good about everything, she didn't even get too upset telling her ma and Nana about what had happened between Melanie and Felecia. She kept the couple of licks she'd taken on behalf of her friend to herself, though. She didn't want the mood spoiled with a mini-lecture about how dangerous it could've been to intervene.

"Poor Melanie" was the topic of discussion at dinner. Sage listened as her Nana and mother talked about the incident, making the same prediction about what would happen as Sage had.

After dinner, Sage went into her room to work on her homework. Her mother took the opportunity to take "a much needed nap" as she always put it. Sage forced herself to concentrate on her homework because of her excitement, but get through it she did.

Chapter 9

As Sage left the apartment in the morning, she was dressed in her favorite jeans and a white tee, with her blue boots. All picked out by Nana; no emergency clothes shoved in her bookbag today! Nana had given her the biggest smile and hug, which Sage returned. Happiness put a spring in her step as she approached the bus stop. As she got closer to Melanie, she was relieved to see her friend at the stop.

"Hey."

"Hey," said Melanie, "you look happy."

"My Nana made me laugh this morning and I'm still thinking about it," replied Sage, still smiling to herself. She noticed Melanie looking down the street while she'd been talking. She looked around too, knowing what had to be on Melanie's mind. "I wonder if Felecia is going to be catching the bus?"

"I don't think so. My mother and I went down to her house last night. My mom told her father what happened and told him she was going to sue him and Felecia for attacking me."

Sage was a little stunned at how matter-of-fact Melanie was about all this. "What did her father say?"

"He didn't say anything. He just stood there and stared. It was weird."

"Did you get a chance to talk to her mother?"

"No, we didn't see her there."

"That's odd." Sage shrugged. At least they hadn't called for Pam to go round there with them. That was something. Sage leant over, dropping her voice. "I'd heard her parents weren't very nice."

"Yeah, that's what we expected. Anyway, my mom told him she was going to take them to court and that you would back up the story."

"What?" Sage's heart jumped up into her throat.

"What do you mean, 'what'?"

"Why would your mother say I would back up your story in court?"

"Because I told her you'd seen everything."

Sage gripped the strap of her book bag and held her friend's gaze. "Melanie, I will tell them exactly what happened, but I'm going to have to tell them everything. That includes the part about why Felecia attacked you to begin with. Did you tell your mother that part?"

Melanie stood there fuming. Sage could actually see her getting angrier by the second.

"No, I didn't tell her about that part. It doesn't matter anyway."

"Why wouldn't it matter?"

"Whose side are you on?" said Melanie loudly. "I only called her names a few times. That was no reason for her to attack me in the middle of the street!"

Sage couldn't believe how blind Melanie was being about how this whole situation arose in the first place. "You picked on her when she was down. You brought up the fact that she was in suspension when she didn't want to talk about it. Plus, you kept enticing her to fight. What do you expect when you give her all this—" Sage pitched her voice high, imitating Melanie. "'Felecia, Fel*eeee*cia', and 'no, *you* got lucky today.'"

"You don't know what you talking about. Saying something to someone is not as bad as hitting somebody."

"It can be, depending on what you say." Sage felt Melanie's furious eyes on her and hated that they were fighting. She took one last shot at putting her own situation across. "Look, you know me. I'm a bad liar. Even if I was happy to go to court and 'forget' about all the stuff you did, some lawyer would dig it out of me in moments, and then you'll look even worse. And I'll get in troub—"

"You know what, Sage?" Melanie grabbed her book bag handle. "If you don't want to be my friend, just say so. First you didn't want to fight Felecia for me and now you're taking her side."

"Yeah!" Sage yelled, as Melanie moved away. "That's why I got hit in the face. Because I'm not your friend. Did you erase that part from your memory, too?"

Sage sucked her teeth and turned her back the other way. She was tired of her friendship being tested every time she tried to get Melanie to see something. Hopefully they'd still be friends once Melanie cooled down, but she was starting to feel too good about herself to get into silly arguments like the ones Melanie had started and would probably always start. Their friendship always seemed to be on Melanie's terms, and Sage was done being pushed around.

For the first time since the school year began, Sage did not sit beside Melanie. Instead, she took Felecia's empty seat. She rode in silence, refusing to let Melanie spoil her good mood.

When they'd arrived at school, Sage picked up her book bag and headed straight to the cafeteria. She picked out some cereal and a carton of milk, took her regular morning seat, put her book bag down, and started opening the cereal. She was the only one at the table for now. As she was pouring the milk, she looked up to see Darren Timberlake walking into the cafeteria with the same student she'd seen him with before. He looked over to Sage and waved. She smiled and waved back. Sage went into her book bag and pulled out the notes she'd put together for her song while she began to eat. She was reviewing them when she heard Darren's voice behind her.

"Hey there Ballerina, mind if we join you?" Darren and the other student were standing there.

"No, I don't mind," she replied with a smile.

"Ballerina, this is Nigel. Nigel, Ballerina."

She shook Nigel's outstretched hand. "Call me Sage."

Darren smiled. "Come on. I like the name Ballerina. Plus, I saw you made the talent show so you must be pretty good."

Sage dug deep for courage and confessed. "Actually…it turns out I really suck at ballet. I made the talent show with the backing music I'd written."

"Really?" Darren folded his arms on the table. "What kind of music do you write?"

"All kinds, whatever I'm feeling at the moment."

"Guess we'll start calling you Keyes."

"I guess you like nicknames," said Sage.

Daren nodded gravely. "I do."

"Then Keyes it is," Sage giggled.

"You'll have to write some music for me one day," Nigel said.

"What do you play?' asked Sage.

"You name it and I'll play it, but mainly the piano and sax."

They spent the rest of the breakfast talking about music and eating. Darren encouraged Sage and Nigel to join the church band, since they were always looking for talent. Nigel had never been to the church, but said he would ask his Dad if they could take him to a service there soon. When the bell rang, Sage and Nigel exchanged numbers and they talked about getting together soon. All the while Darren stood there in the background, grinning from ear to ear as if he was watching his favorite children playing nicely at Sunday school. They said their good-byes and walked away.

Sage headed to homeroom with her head in the clouds. Nigel was not just a musician interested in Sage's talents. He was also fine! She got to homeroom and got herself settled into her seat, so pleased she'd been straight up with Darren about not doing ballet well. It hadn't even mattered; he'd just quickly gone on to her real talents and nicknamed her for Alicia Keyes, whom her friends knew and loved. Had she been honest with herself and others when she first tried out for the talent show, she probably would not have had so much embarrassment to begin with.

Sage's homeroom teacher was Mr. Crumpwell for English. As he started talking through the day's lesson, she pulled out her homework assignment and looked to her right, where another student was just sitting and smiling at her. Odd. Nice, but odd. Turning back to look at Mr. Crumpwell, she noticed him smiling at her, too. It finally dawned on Sage that everyone was smiling at her because she herself couldn't stop smiling

Chapter 10

The school day had been great, apart from the silence between her and Melanie. She wanted to tell Melanie all about breakfast and Nigel, but didn't want to give in so easily. They were riding home on the bus now, still in separate seats. They'd seen each other a few times during school and had kept walking without speaking to one another. Two of Sage's other friends had noticed and asked what was wrong between the two of them. Sage had said nothing and left it at that. As Sage got off the bus and began walking home, she secretly hoped Melanie would call out her name and apologize for what she'd said. But she didn't hear anything so she kept walking like she just didn't care.

When she got home, she and her Nana spent time together like they always did. Nana had a nice snack prepared and they talked about school. After they'd talked for a while, Sage pulled out her music to practice. She'd just started flicking through her new notes when she heard the phone ring. She reached for the phone, but her Nana had already gotten it. She heard her Nana telling someone to hold on. She held out the receiver with a sly smile on her face.

Sage walked over and took the phone from her Nana's hand. "Hello?"

"Hi Sage, it's Nigel."

"Hi!!"

Nana chuckled and moved to to someplace else in the house. Sage blushed at being so obviously excited to hear from him, but talking to

Nigel was easy and they went on and on. Finally, he admitted to having homework he needed to do, and they got off the phone. As soon as Sage put the phone on the cradle, her Nana reappeared.

"Who was that, Baby?"

"This boy I met at school today. He plays a lot of instruments like me and wants me to write some music for him."

Nana smiled and shook her head. "The good Lord is making things happen for you Sage. Of course, you make it a lot easier for him when you see what gifts he has to bring."

"I know, Nana," Sage said, smiling. "Thank you."

Just as Sage was giving her a hug, someone knocked on the door. Nana went to answer the door as Sage stood behind her. There stood a worn-out looking man. Sage knew who it was before he even introduced himself—there was more than a little resemblance between Felicia Finch and her father.

"I apologize for bothering you, but I wondered if you might have a moment to talk?" he asked. "My name is Mr. Finch and my daughter, Felecia, goes to school with your daughter."

"Granddaughta, but come on in and have a sit down."

Nana showed Mr. Finch to the kitchen table, offering him a snack and a glass of water, which he accepted. As they talked, Sage thought he didn't look mean or nothing. Just tired.

Mr. Finch began talking, sharing he was frightened by the threat of a lawsuit against his daughter. He wanted to speak with Sage, since she'd been at the fight. His biggest concern was whether Felecia could make it through such an ordeal. Had someone said that to Sage a day ago, she would have bet money Felecia could make it through just about anything.

It turned out that Felecia's mother had gotten very sick two years ago and had passed away from her illness at the end of last school semester.

Apparently, Felecia's mother didn't take her sickness or the possibility of departing this earth too well. They'd moved from their previous neighborhood when Felecia's mom insisted they move in order to have a fresh start, but the move put extra strain on her, making her worse.

"She was such a good and strong person and a great mother," Mr. Finch paused, turning his glass of water round and around. "She did everything for Felecia. Made sure her schoolin' was taken care of, her diet, medicine, all her doctor's appointments." He paused again, then continued.

"Felecia had been so social and lively, always interested in fashion. She's bipolar, but with her medicine she always did well. You wouldn't even know; except when they change the dosage and she gets sleepy." Mr. Finch went on to blame himself; there had been so much to do when Mrs. Finch got sick that he didn't have time to put into Felecia, thought she was taking her medicines and then the move cut her off from her friends.

Sage and her Nana were speechless for a while, until Sage spoke up. "Mr. Finch, I can speak with Melanie and her mother about this lawsuit. They are upset, but I'm pretty sure they wouldn't go through with anything once they've heard your story."

"That'd be kind." His shoulders slumped. "I sure hope it works."

Sage thought about telling him what Melanie had done to provoke Felecia, but it didn't seem to matter at this point. Apparently, Felecia had been in several fights and had issues bigger than her fight with Melanie.

"Really, thank you so much for your time." He gave a tired smile and headed out, moving even more slowly than when he'd walked in. He handed her a card with his number on it. "Please would you let me know how it goes?"

The moment he left, Sage looked at her Nana. "I think I need to go see Melanie and her parents. Now. Would you come with me?"

"You know what Sage means? It means 'wise'. That's you, girl. That's the real you." Nana kissed her on the cheek. "I'll just get my coat."

* * * *

"Oh, my." Mrs James put her tea back on the table and bit her lip. "That's just…awful. Okay, simple answer—we won't even consider pressing a lawsuit."

"I'll go over myself and apologize," Mr. James assured. "I didn't give the man a chance to speak."

Sage had caught Melanie's eyes several times while the adults spoke. She could tell by her look that they were no longer mad at one another. If anything, Melanie looked a little ashamed.

Sage and her Nana got up to leave and Mr. James walked them to the door. After they'd said their good-byes, Sage grabbed Nana's arm and locked it into hers. After hearing about Felecia's story, she was determined not take her Nana or mother for granted. They walked arm and arm all the way back home.

Chapter 11

Sage was on the stage playing her heart out. She sat on a high chair in her long denim skirt with tan leather boots. She had a blond colored linen shirt on with her mother's tan hat to top it off. The hall lights were dimmed, with the stage lights shining directly on Sage, who felt like she was the only person in the room. She pressed the saxophone against her lips and made the music swell as it filled the room with sounds unheard of. She was so wrapped into the music that all she could see was darkness. She played and played until '*Patricia*' wound down to its finish.

The name definitely fitted the song.

Sage opened her eyes and placed the saxophone on her lap. It was so quiet in the room, she found herself rubbing her neck like she always did when she was nervous. Then the lights came on and she began to hear claps. Claps so loud they were deafening. She looked out into the audience and people were standing.

Sage blinked her eyes to wake herself up, but this was no dream. She was actually getting a standing ovation. As the lights came up further, she peered into the talent show audience to see her Nana and mother sitting right in front, beaming. Her mother held a digital camera with one hand and waved with the other. Sage waved back and began to walk off the stage.

Nigel snuck out from behind the curtain and gave her a big hug, snatching her off her feet. "You are *awesome*, girl!"

Sage giggled, not knowing what to say.

Melanie came over and gave her a big hug as well. "Didn't I tell you you'd be the bomb?"

"Keyes!!" Darren walked up saying, hand to his mouth and smiling. "You were amazing!"

Sage gave them all high fives, still a little floaty with disbelief. She'd had actually been the last act in the show, which had been fine with her. She had been lucky enough to be considered again. As she walked out through the audience, people either congratulated her or stared at her in amazement.

She managed to make it past everyone and get to her Nana and mother, who were waiting at the back. She gave them both tight hugs, feeling tears in her eyes to match those in her Nana's.

"Your auntie Pat would feel so honored you named that beautiful song after her."

Her mom hugged her too and reached up to give her a kiss on the cheeks. "I've decided there's too much sleeping in my life. You've got to teach me how to play that thing. There *has* to be a musical bone in me somewhere."

Sage laughed, still walking on air.

Nigel squeezed through the crowd to tell her he had to leave, but he'd call her over the weekend. Sage felt herself going red in the face, and even redder as Melanie came over with her parents, all of them grinning and bouncing their eyebrows as Nigel squeezed Sage's hand and then took off.

"We spoke with Mr. Finch," Mr. James reported. "It went as well as could've been expected. And…" he cast a fond look downwards. "Melanie admitted to upsetting Felecia and apologized for picking on her."

Sage gathered Melanie into a huge hug. "You go, girl. I'm proud of you."

"I got there. Eventually." Melanie laughed and pulled Sage to one side. "You know what's really good? I had this long talk with mom and dad when we got home. Well, it started out as a fight, but I told them stuff I hadn't said for months, like I was tired of coming home the moment the bell rang. There's movies and skate parties everybody goes to and I can't. Life isn't all school, sleep, church and praying."

"What?!" You actually went there with them? How did they respond?

"I'm going to get some free time on Saturdays and can go to the movies on Fridays!" she squealed, unable to contain her excitement at her new found hours of freedom.

Sage laughed. "So…what are you going to do with all this free time?"

"More movies, shopping, even the library ALONE sounds dope!" Melanie giggled. "I'll take this freedom thing one step at a time."

Sage looped her arm around Melanie's neck. Finally, everything seemed right.

She thought back to everything she'd been through over the last couple weeks and chuckled to herself. If someone had told her life could be like this the day she was in the church yard telling Darren Timberlake she knew ballet, she wouldn't have believed it. It had all been within her grasp all along. All she'd needed to do was love herself, love her talents and… add a little bit of honesty.

Mr. James clapped hands and rubbed them together. "It's Friday night and we can't seem to stop talking, so how about everyone come over to our place for pizza?"

"Yeh!" Melanie and Sage yelled in unison.

"I'm going to call Mr. Finch and invite him and Felecia. I'm not sure they can come, but we're going to do everything possible to reach out to them. They've been through an awful lot."

"Amen to that," said Nana.

Sage and Melanie walked behind the adults as they all headed out of the auditorium.

"Sage, you have to tell me about Nigel!"

"So, the interrogation begins, huh?" Sage giggled, happy to give in. She just turned to look back up at the stage one more time.

What a way to start your new beginning.

Patricia, we're on our way.

DISCUSSION QUESTIONS

1. Describe Sage based on qualities and characteristics you find in the book. In your description, provide examples of Sage's responses when people comment on her looks and talents. What kind of self-image do you think she has at the beginning of the book? Explain your answer.

2. When Sage is asked by Darren Timberlake if she is participating in the school talent show, she tells a lie about her talents. Because Darren seems impressed, she begins to fantasize about how she can make the lie become a reality. What lengths does Sage go through to make this happen? Sage's time line is only a few days. Is her attempt to turn this fantasy into reality realistic? What time line might be more realistic and why?

3. Discuss the advice Sage gives to her friend, Melanie James, and the advice her friend gives to her throughout the book. In your discussion, include whether you think Sage and Melanie are positive or negative peer models. Consider and discuss why both Sage and Melanie are able to provide advice to one another, but may not recognize their own circumstances.

4. Two of the characters, Melanie James and Felecia Finch, exhibit risky and harmful behaviors. Identify what some of these behaviors are. Discuss your perception of why they are exhibiting such behaviors and what you think they feel they may gain from it.

5. Towards the end of the story, we learn that Felecia Finch suffers from a mental illness which is complicated by a traumatic experience. How could Sage and Melanie have learned about this earlier? Is there anything Melanie could have done differently before the situation escalated to a fight? Discuss these options.

6. Discuss the following relationships that exist in the book. In your discussion, indicate whether or not these relationships are considered positive or not so positive. Include traits or comments that support your responses. Discuss whether or not the relationships changed at the end of the story. Relationships: Sage and Foster. Melanie and her parents. Sage and her mother. Sage and her grandmother. Sage and Melanie. Melanie and Felecia. Felecia and Sage. Sage and Darren. Sage and Nigel.

7. Did you identify any adult positive role models in the book? If so, who are they? What traits and qualities do they exhibit that make them a positive role model? In contrast, were there any negative role models? If so, who are they? What traits and characteristics do they exhibit that make them a negative role model?

8. Discuss the ending. What is your perception of Sage's image at the end of the story in contrast to the beginning of the story? What is your perception of the friendship between her and Melanie James?

NOTES

NOTES

NOTES

 # NOTES

The LOVE, RELATIONSHIPS AND YOU GAME

The Love, Relationships and You game centers around principles that can help make decisions around day to day situations we come across in our lives. The principles fall under sub-headings that have been aligned with letters from L, O, V, E, N, O, T, E.

GAME INSTRUCTIONS

1. Start by reading through the list of principles on pages 82 and 83. We encourage you to discuss the principles with family and friends. Definitions can be found on pages 84 with scripture references found on pages 85-86.

2. Beginning on page. 87, you will see a list of categories. Each category is worth the total number of points listed to its right. Points are obtained by answering three questions from each of categories.

3. Questions start on page 88 with the first category "Me and Me" and end on page 97 with the last category "Don't Always Believe What You Hear." Place your answers from each question in the corresponding number found in the matching category box located at the bottom of each page.

For example:

Me and Me

1. You have a crush on someone. You over hear that the person you have a crush on only likes people who buys them things. You:

    a. Break open the piggy bank and buy them something nice.

    b. Find out what they like first, then break open the piggy bank and buy them something nice.

    c. Don't buy them anything. That's not a good way to start a relationship.

Me and Me For

(15 Points)

1. a

2.

3.

---

4. Once all questions are answered, tally up your answers by using the answer key located on page 98 and place your total score on page 99.

GROUND RULES

Learn

There are no wrong answers

If more than one person is playing, only one speaks at a time Have

fun

Love is (Patient), Love is (Kind), it is not puffed up
or arrogant (Humble), it does not act unbecomingly
(Respectful), it does not seek its own (Selfless), it does not
rejoice in unrighteousness, but rejoices in truth (Honest), it
bears all things, endures all things, it never
fails (Committed). .... 1 *Corinthians* 13:4-8a

*"My great hope is to laugh as much as I cry; to get my work done
nd try to love somebody and the courage to accept the love in return."
– Maya Angelou*

PRINCIPLES

L   Love Yourself and Others (Respectful)

1. Walk, speak, dress and carry yourself with love and grace; honoring your body at all times; even when others aren't looking.

2. Value and respect others in a light brighter than the one you see yourself with.

3. Be open-minded and respectful of differences.

O   Open Your Heart to Honesty (Honest)

4. Be honest, sincere and genuine about who you are, what you like and don't like and where you are from.

5. Tell the truth in and of all things.

6. Help others to be honest through the pursuit of truth and right ideas.

V   Visualize Your Future (Patience)

7. See past any and all limitations, envisioning a good and strong future.

8. Seek out relationships and wisdom (teachers, guidance counselors and positive family members) who can support and provide guidance towards what you hope to achieve.

9. Stay steadfast and courageous in your plans to grow and master your talents and gifts.

E   Expect Fair Treatment (Fairness)

10. Be fair and impartial.

11. Expect others to treat you fairly, setting boundaries and requiring others to be accountable when they don't treat you fairly.

12. If you are not being treated fairly, humbly excuse yourself and seek company that will treat you fairly.

N   Nurture Friendships (Committed)

13. Keep your true friends' interest at heart.

14. Be generous and ensure you are not taking family, friends and associates for granted.

15. Ask for and give forgiveness.

O   Observe and Favor Quiet Strength (Humble)

16. Listen to what people say or don't say.

17. Watch how people treat other people, how they carry themselves and what they practice.

18. Spend less time trying to be interesting and more time being interested.

T   Take Ownership of Your Actions (Selfless)

19. Listen to, take care of and own the words that come out of your mouth.

20. Accept mistakes and apologize when others are affected by it.

21. Do everything possible to keep peace.

E   Express Positive Thinking (Kind)

22. Keep a positive outlook, pursuing unity and peace.

23. Don't think the worst of people and don't stereotype. Add value to others.

24. Be grateful.

DEFINITIONS

L   Love Yourself and Others (Respectful)

Respectful. Full of, characterized by, or showing politeness or deference.

O   Open Your Heart to Honesty (Honest)

Honest. Honorable in principles, intentions, and actions. Upright and fair.

V   Visualize Your Future (Patience)

Patience. The quality of being patient, without complaint, loss of temper, irritation or

E   Expect Fair Treatment (Fairness)

Fairness. Free from bias or injustice; evenhandedness.

N   Nurture Friendships (Committed)

Committed. Dedication and loyalty to a cause, activity or job

O   Observe and Favor Quiet Strength (Humble)

Humble. Not proud or arrogant; modest.

T   Take Ownership of Your Actions (Selfless)

Selfless. More concerned with the needs and wishes of others than with one's own self; unselfish.

E   Express Positive Thinking (Kind)

Kind. Having or showing a friendly, generous and considerate nature.

SCRIPTURE REFERENCES

L
Love Yourself and Others (Respectful)

1. Walk, speak, dress and carry yourself with love and grace; honoring your body at all times; even when others aren't looking [Romans 12:1-2]

2. Value and respect others in a light brighter than the one you see yourself with [Romans 12:3-8]

3. Be open-minded and respectful of differences. [1 Peter 3:8-12]

O
Open Your Heart to Honesty (Honest)

4. Be honest, sincere and genuine about who you are, what you like and don't like and where you are from. [2 Corinthians 4:2]

5. Tell the truth in and of all things. [Leviticus 19:11]

6. Help others to be honest through the pursuit of truth and right ideas. [Philippians 4:8-9]

V
Visualize Your Future (Patience)

7. See past any and all limitations, envisioning a good and strong future. [Philippians 4:13]

8. Seek out relationships and wisdom (teachers, guidance counselors and positive family members) who can support and provide guidance towards what you hope to achieve. [Proverbs 4:5-13]

9. Stay steadfast and courageous in your plans to grow and master your talents and gifts. [1 Timothy 4:12-14]

E
Expect Fair Treatment (Fairness)

10. Be fair and impartial. [James 2:1-4]

11. Expect others to treat you fairly, setting boundaries and requiring others to be accountable when they don't treat you fairly. [Isaiah 1:17]

12. If you are not being treated fairly, humbly excuse yourself and seek company that will treat you fairly. [Proverbs 4:4-19]

N   Nurture Friendships (Committed)

13. Keep your true friends' interest at heart [Philippians 2:4]

14. Be generous and ensure you are not taking family, friends and associates for granted [Proverbs 11:25].

15. Ask for and give forgiveness [Luke 6:37]

O   Observe and Favor Quiet Strength (Humble)

16. Listen to what people say or don't say [James 1:19].

17. Watch how people treat other people, how they carry themselves and what they practice. [2 Peter 2:1-3]

18. Spend less time trying to be interesting and more time being interested. [Proverbs 16:1-2]

T   Take Ownership of Your Actions (Selfless)

19. Listen to, take care of and own the words that come out of your mouth [Proverbs 10:31-32].

20. Accept mistakes and apologize when others are affected by it [2 Timothy 22-24].

21. Do everything possible to keep peace [Romans 12:18].

E   Express Positive Thinking (Kind)

22. Keep a positive outlook, pursuing faith, unity and peace. [2 Peter 1:5-8]

23. Don't think the worst of people and don't stereotype. Add value to others [Romans 13:8-10].

24. Be grateful [Philippians 4:11-12].

CATEGORIES	
Category Group	Number of Points
Me and Me	15
Boys, Girls and Crushes	30
Crushes and Me	15
The Triangle	15
Crushes & Phone Calls	15
The Blame Game	30
Shared Feelings	15
Feelings & Trust	15
The Note	15
Don't Always Believe What You Hear	30

Me and Me

1. You have a crush on someone. You over hear that the person you have a crush on only likes people who buys them things. You:

    a. Break open the piggy bank and buy them something nice.

    b. Find out what they like first, then break open the piggy bank and buy them something nice.

    c. Don't buy them anything. That's not a good way to start a relationship.

2. The person you like LOVES a sport you do not care for. Do you;

    a. Pretend like you really like the sport. After all, you gotta do what you gotta do to get and keep their attention.

    b. Start buying and wearing the sports team's jerseys and paraphernalia around school.

    c. Ask them to share interesting things about the sport to learn more about it.

3. The person you like LOVES long hair and your hair is short. Do you;

    a. Work for extra allowance money so you can go buy some weave.

    b. Become sad and depressed because you don't have what it takes to get their attention.

    c. Move on to someone else. They have a right to like what they like and there are other people who won't focus on one attribute.

Me and Me For
(15 Points)

1.

2.

3.

Boys, Girls and Crushes

4. When someone you like responds to a text you send, does it mean they like you back?

    a. Yes, why else would they take the time to respond to your text.

    b. Not necessarily, they may just be trying to get to know you.

    c. I don't know; more information is needed.

5. Which gender thinks about the other the most?

    a. Boys

    b. Girls

    c. I don't know; more information is needed.

6. Do you think all boys want to have a girlfriend? Do you think all girls want to have a boyfriend?

    a. Yes, everyone should have a soulmate.

    b. Yes, if they don't have one, people will begin to wonder.

    c. No, having a significant other is not the most important thing at our age.

Boys, Girls & Crushes For
(30 Points)

4.

5.

6.

Crushes and Me

7. A person you don't like, really likes you. Do you:

   a. Avoid them like the plague and hope they go away.

   b. If the opportunity comes up, let them know as nicely as possible you are not interested.

   c. Have your friend tell them you're not interested so you won't have to.

8. You're popular, but you like someone that everyone thinks is whacky. Do you;

   a. Act like you think they are whacky too.

   b. Let them know you like them. Who cares what other people think.

   c. Date them secretly. After all, you don't want to lose your popularity.

9. You like someone, but you don't know if they like you. Do you;

   a. Pay attention to how they act around you before doing anything.

   b. Ask your friend to ask them if they like you.

   c. Find one of their friends and ask them if they've heard anything about them liking you.

Crushes and Me For

(15 Points)

7.

8.

9.

The Triangle

10. Two of your friends like the same person. The person they like comes to you one day and asks you out! You kind of like the idea of going out with them. Do you:

    a. Go out with them in secret and hope your friends don't find out.

    b. Let the person know you are honored, but can't accept their invitation because you are close to someone who has a crush on them.

    c. Tell your friends you've been asked out and if they aren't hurt by it, go out with the person.

11. A person is making your school days unpleasant because they like someone they see you with all the time. Do you:

    a. Approach them and tell them they better leave you alone.

    b. Tell your friends to confront them for you and tell them they better leave you alone.

    c. Let a school official know.

12. The person you really like, likes someone else. Do you:

    a. Spread rumors about the other person. Once the person you like hears the rumors, they won't like them anymore.

    b. Like them secretly since they don't have the same feelings for you.

    c. Like them for who they are and move on with your school, activities and life. There are other fish in the sea.

The Triangle For
(15 Points)

10.

11.

12.

Crushes and Phone Calls

13. Your friend wants to hook you up with somebody on the phone. Do you:

    a. Let them because you need somebody anyway.

    b. Say no because you can handle your own hook ups.

    c. Ask questions about the person they have in mind so you can make an informed decision.

14. Your friend calls you upset. They are having trouble with their significant other and want you to do a three-way phone call with them. Do you:

    a. Get on the call and yell at your friend's significant other for making your friend upset.

    b. Make up a story that you can't because you don't want to do it.

    c. Explain to your friend you can listen and provide support, but the issue is between the two of them.

15. You receive a phone call from an angry person. They are yelling at you about someone you like who they say is their significant other. Do you:

    a. Yell at them back.

    b. Once they stop yelling, be direct and tell them you won't speak to someone who is yelling and let them know you are hanging up the phone.

    c. Start speaking another language so they think they have the wrong number.

Crushes & Phone Calls For
(15 Points)

13.

14.

15.

The Blame Game

16. The most popular person in school is always walking past the person you like. Do you:

    a. Tell your friends they need to stop trying to get the attention of the person you like.

    b. Walk by the person you like just as much. They may be popular, but you've got style.

    c. Do nothing. People are walking through school every day. You are exaggerating.

17. Your friend tells a boy/girl you like them AFTER you told them not to. The person responds they don't like you back. Do you:

    a. Blame your friend. You told them not to say anything and now it's messed up.

    b. Realize it's better to know now rather than later, but discuss the betrayal of your trust with your friend.

    c. Tell the boy/girl your friend was lying.

18. The boy/girl you've liked forever just asked for your phone number so they could call you tonight. When they call, it's very late and you are sleeping when you hear it ring. Do you:

    a. Tell them you were sleeping and ask if its' OK for you all to talk tomorrow.

    b. Let the call go to voice mail.

    c. Pick up the call and act like you were up.

The Blame Game For
(30 Points)

16.

17.

18.

Shared Feelings

19. Your friend dated someone who now wants to date you. Your friend tells you not to go out with them. Do you:
    a. Go out with them in secret.
    b. Date them and let your friend know about your decision.
    c. Listen to your friend and leave them alone.

20. You find out the person you are dating is dating someone else. You:
    a. Confront the other person they are dating.
    b. Act like you don't know and keep going with the person. They are worth it.
    c. Let them know you need time apart or possibly end the relationship since they are dishonest.

21. You find out two of your close friends are dating the same boy/girl, but your friends don't know it. Do you:
    a. Tell them both. They deserve to know the truth.
    b. Go tell the boy/girl you know what's going on and he/she'd better break it off with one of them.
    c. Stay quiet. After all, two's company, three's a crowd and a fourth wheel only sounds good on T.V.

Shared Feelings For
(15 Points)
19.
20.
21.

Feelings and Trust

22. Your best friend has just revealed they have a crush on someone you like. Should you:
    a. Be happy for them and move on to someone else.
    b. Share you also have a crush on that person and now you two can't be 'besties.'
    c. Share you also have a crush and then laugh about the possibility the person might not like either one of you.

23. A close friend secretly shares they have a crush on someone. Do you;
    a. Listen and keep confidences.
    b. Only tell your best friend because they like the same person and need to know.
    c. Tell your cousin in another state because you have to tell someone and they live so far away no one will ever care.

24. You tell a boy/girl that you like them and ask them not to tell anyone. They start telling everyone and you hear about it. Do you;
    a. Deny it and act like they are lying.
    b. Ignore him/her and share with people you did like them until they showed how inconsiderate they truly are.
    c. Act like you don't feel well so you can avoid school until it all blows over.

Feelings & Trust For
(15 Points)

22.

23.

24.

The Note

25. You find a note in the school yard. It was written by a boy/girl you don't like to a boy/girl you do like. Do you:
    a. Change the name to yours. It's a pretty good note so you might as well use it.
    b. Give the note to the boy/girl it was intended for. It's a good way to get to close to him/her.
    c. Give the note back to the person who wrote it and explain it was in the yard.

26. Your friend wants you to deliver a note to the boy/girl they really like. They want you to deliver it in the cafeteria. Do you:
    a. Take the note, but tell your friend you will deliver it someplace where there are less people.
    b. Tell them they'll have to deliver the note themselves and advise them not to deliver it where there are a lot of people watching.
    c. Act like you are going to deliver the note, but then spill some food on it so you won't have to.

27. You write a note to someone you really like and want to get it to them without a whole lot of people knowing. Do you:
    a. Go up to them when no one is around and hand it to them.
    b. Ask your best, best friend to give it to them. You know for sure they won't tell anyone.
    c. Tear the note up. You don't have the guts to give it to them.

The Note For
(15 Points)

25.

26.

27.

Don't Always Believe What You Hear

28. You hear from some people the most popular person in school likes you. Do you:

    a. Ask them if they like you and risk them saying no.

    b. Tell your friends to ask the friend of the popular person if they like you.

    c. Don't pay attention to the rumors. If they like you, they will tell you.

29. You hear from some people, that your boy/girl friend is getting ready to break up with you for someone else. Do you:

    a. Go find him/her in the hallway and tell them off.

    b. Break up with them before they can break up with you.

    c. Don't react to the rumors.

30. Somebody told somebody who told you that your boy/girlfriend was at the movies with someone else. Do you:

    a. Act like you were at the movies and saw them there when you confront him/her about what you heard.

    b. Call the movie theatre to see if they have video clips of people coming in and out of the theatre.

    c. Tell your boyfriend/girlfriend one of your friends saw them at the theatre. Ask them what they saw and based on what they say, you'll decide what to do next.

Don't Always Believe What You Hear For

(30 Points)

28.

29.

30.

Me and Me
For (15 Points)
1. c = 5

2. c = 5

3. c = 5

Boys, Girls & Crushes
For (30 Points)
4. b = 10

5. b = 10

6. c = 10

Crushes and Me
For (15 Points)
7. c = 5

8. b = 5

9. a = 5

The Triangle
For (15 Points)
10. c = 5

11. a = 5

12. c = 5

Crushes & Phone Calls For (15 Points)
13. d = 5

14. c = 5

15. b = 5

The Blame Game
For (30 Points)
16. c = 10

17. b = 10

18. a = 10

Shared Feelings
For (15 Points)
19. c = 5

20. c = 5

21. a = 5

Feelings & Trust
For (15 Points)
22. c = 5

23. a = 5

24. b = 5

The Note
For (15 Points)
25. c = 5

26. c = 5

27. a = 5

Don't Always Believe What You Hear For (30 Points)
28. c = 10

29. c = 10

30. d = 10

Total: _____

Up to 65 **Nice! Keep playing with family and friends.**

66 – 130 **Good Job! You are becoming a model for goodness!**

131 – 195 **Excellent! You'll do a great job teaching these principles to others.**

ABOUT THE AUTHOR

Mechelle Esparza- Harris is a lifelong advocate for the education, safety and welfare of children and young adults. From serving on the Board of Directors for an adoption agency, tutoring children at risk for failing in the Richmond and Henrico Virginia school system to being a Court Appointed Special Advocate serving the Henrico County Domestic and Juvenile Court System, she has a passion for ensuring, when given the chance, she makes a positive imprint on a young person's life. As a creative writer, she has written several poems and received the Editor's Choice Award for Outstanding Achievement in Poetry awarded by The National Library of Poetry. She has two published young adult books and one published children's illustrated book. Mechelle's work career has included being a flight attendant for Delta Air Lines to working for over twenty-five years in commercial underwriting and risk management for both an insurance company and governmental agency. She absolutely loves being a wife, mother, daughter, sister, friend and aunt to a host of nieces, nephews and non-biological children she calls her own including her four-legged pups and grand-pups.

OTHER BOOKS BY MECHELLE ESPARZA-HARRIS

"The Love Note," **Second edition.**

"… This book will teach young people to listen to your gut instincts and not to crack under pressure. Always be willing to stand up for what is right and the importance of valuing true friendship. I also love the relationship the main character has with her parents ..."

Amazon Customer March 2019

"… Your book, "The Love Note" should be in every Junior High School. In fact, it should be required 7th grade reading."

Millie Preston, Retired Educator, New York City, NY

"… I loved this book and how my niece's eyes lit up. I work for and run a maternity home for college age women. I spoke to them about the book and they loved the idea of introducing children to college through a puppy's eyes. I hope this book gets to all public schools. We need to instill in children that college is possible. The earlier we reach them, the more motivated and excited they will be about pursuing a college degree."

Tracey Questell, Healing Vine Harbor

www.ingramcontent.com/pod-product-compliance
Lightning Source LLC
Chambersburg PA
CBHW030354180626
46812CB00007B/2872